MR WILMOTT GETS OLD SCHOOL

CHARITY SHOP HAUNTED MYSTERY BOOK TWO

KATHERINE HAYTON

MR WILMOTT GETS OLD SCHOOL

ISBN: 978-0-9951007-4-9

*E*mily Curtis stood up, her knees popping like firecrackers, then lost her balance and collapsed. She broke into giggles as Maude, a white English Bulldog with questionable hygiene, launched at her and covered her face with long licks of her rough tongue.

"Enough," she called out, her nose full of dog. She snorted as Maude then bumped her snout into the crease between her shoulder and ear. With her pug nose, the bulldog's breathing was loud at the best of times. Close up to Emily's ear, it sounded like a pair of bellows wet from the rain.

"Do you need a hand?" Gregory asked, towering above her. His right eyebrow launched upwards but given its speed, the conversation would have moved on before it quite got where it was going.

"No. Just back up a little, Maude, and I'll try that again."

This time, when Emily stood, her knees offered the same sound effect, but momentum won the fight against gravity. "Remind me not to kneel again," she said, stretching out one leg, then the other, to get them working. "All the physio in the world won't compete with age."

"I don't know what you're talking about," Agnes Myrtle said as she came into the room holding an old filigree lamp. "I've got twenty years on you, and I can still kneel just fine when I'm gardening."

"It's not the kneeling. It's the getting back up."

The two women smiled at each other, then Agnes gave a sigh and extended the light to Emily. "Is this worth anything? My father was obsessed with gold filigree and this is one of the better examples he bought home from overseas."

Overseas meant the second world war. Although Emily had only met the woman for the first time that day, she'd already heard many tales of Agnes's dad's adventures fighting in Africa. Although the woman hadn't been born until a few years after he returned, the conflict had featured large in her childhood home life.

"It's in beautiful shape," Emily said, taking the lamp and examining it from all angles. "No cracks or discolouration."

"Is that the nice way of saying it's worthless?"

"Valueless, not worthless." Emily handed it back. "If it means something to you, I'd recommend you keep it. If not, we'll be able to get a small sum at auction."

Agnes stroked the old fabric of the shade and turned the body of the object toward the window to catch the sun. "I'll leave it in the maybe pile. Until I get all the *definitely going* stuff moved into the unit, I won't know if I've got room spare or not."

Gregory and Emily were packing up Agnes's life worth

of possessions, preparatory to moving her into the local retirement home and hospital complex, Stoneybrook Acres. The charity shop offered the service in return for the donation of goods not able to fit into the smaller space.

Although their help was warranted, the back of Emily's neck tingled as she examined treasured objects and offered a verdict under the gaze of the owner. She might be an avid watcher of Antique's Roadshow, but it hadn't prepared her for the emotional turmoil of delivering her appraisal, knowing it might hurt.

Opening boxes and examining their contents in the airless room above the charity shop was relaxing in comparison.

"I'll take these out to the car," Gregory announced, pulling a box off the kitchen bench. "The first test will be fitting them into your little hatchback. If we can squeeze in all these *and* fit a driver, it'll be a miracle."

Emily wrinkled her nose as the young man sloped out to her vehicle. She wanted to retort her little vehicle was much roomier than his non-existent one but was wary of discussing cars. Being unable to afford one while at university had led Gregory onto a path decidedly not straight and narrow.

One more jibe from him, and she couldn't be held responsible though. Even a nice old woman like herself had a limit.

"Maude, get your nose out of there," Agnes scolded from the kitchen. "How's it going to look when your new family gets here if you've coated your muzzle in icing sugar?"

The dog sneezed and Emily resisted the urge to poke her head around the corner and view the unfolding drama.

The woman might hide it well, but there was a catch in Agnes's voice as she spoke to her beloved pet. The retirement community didn't allow the residents to have dogs. After eight years of keeping her mistress company, Maude was about to be rehoused.

"One down," Gregory said as he walked back inside the house. He flicked his blond fringe back from his hazel eyes and scanned the room as though entering for the first time.

Over the months Emily had worked with him, she'd grown used to the faint air of puzzlement that accompanied the young man into every situation. The slowest moving person she'd ever met, it had taken her a while to realise Gregory wasn't lazy. He just moved to a different rhythm.

The confused expression lifted, as it always did, and he sauntered toward the next box in line.

"Be extra careful with that one," Emily said with a frown. "It's got Agnes's best treasures."

Treasure was the word Agnes had been using and Emily had adopted it over the last few hours. It fitted much better than possessions or goods. The emotional attachment the woman had to the different objects in her house exposed a sentimentality far higher than Emily was used to.

She didn't want to imagine how it must feel to the woman to give up such belongings but couldn't stop herself. The pain written across Agnes's face appeared akin to stripping skin from flesh.

Every item had been a gift or a hand-me-down, an inheritance from every relative and friend who'd loomed large in the woman's life. To tear her apart from these items stuffed full of emotional memories was cruel.

Emily shivered, though she stood in a patch of warm sunlight.

Soon it might be her turn to lose her home and her

possessions. She didn't want to feel the loss any sooner than necessary, but her empathy kept bubbling up to the surface, wanting to take part.

At least a retirement facility couldn't object to her cat, Peanut. A ghost pet flew under the radar of even the most intense scrutiny.

"There you go," Agnes told Maude. "All clean again. Now, don't you go getting into any more trouble before your new family arrives. I've got enough to do without chasing after you every minute."

Emily listened as the dog paced the length of the kitchen, her nails clicking off the tiled surface. Perhaps she should transport the first load of boxes to the retirement village with Gregory now and let Agnes have alone-time with her dog.

As though her thought had triggered the question, Agnes walked into the lounge with a worried expression. "I wonder if I should give Maude's new family a call. They're running a few minutes late."

"They might be stuck in traffic somewhere," Emily said. "Did you say they had children?"

Agnes nodded. "Two daughters. Maude is going to love having children to run around with after years of being stuck with a slowcoach." She bent and wrinkled her nose at the dog who stared back with an adoring expression. To Emily, it didn't appear Maude wanted any changes.

"If they've got children, you can expect them to run late." Emily smiled as she thought of the multitude of families who'd missed appointments in her old diary.

As an accountant, she'd billed by the minute whether the client turned up for their appointment or not. To give back to the community, though, she'd volunteered time and budget advice at the local citizen's advice bureau.

A lot of those scheduled meetings had been pushed back as the realities of organising a family into a car for the journey took a toll. Harried parents spending every last cent on their beloved progeny were a common sight.

At the start of Emily's career, two full-time jobs had always supplied an adequate lifestyle. By the end, the ridiculous housing market had squeezed even those couples down a bracket.

"I hope she forgives me," Agnes said, her voice so thick with tears it took Emily a moment to untangle the words.

"Maude?"

The older woman nodded. "When I picked her up from the dog pound, I said I'd take care of her for as long as I had breath in my body. And now…"

Emily turned away. Her stomach was already a tight knot of tension. She didn't want to watch Agnes cry. "Now, she's moving into a new place with a loving family and she'll still remember you and be grateful every day of her life."

Maude pulled away from Agnes and trotted into the kitchen, displaying the tight swirl of her tail. Again, her toenails clacked on the tiles as she paced back and forth in the room.

Emily followed the dog and when Maude passed by on one of her patrol circuits, gave her a pat. A quiver ran through her hand—the dog shaking. The poor thing must know something was happening. Like a baby fussing when their mother is upset, the dog paced and shook while her owner cried.

She wanted to be anywhere but inside the household. Gregory stood out by her car, chatting on his phone to somebody. He was either oblivious to the situation indoors or escaping it.

Lucky thing.

Pain arced through Emily's body. Not the physical kind, she was used to that. Following a car accident the year before, she'd found her limits of endurance were far higher than she'd ever imagined. This was an emotional pain, tied up with fear.

Fear that in a year's time, or two, it might be her sorting through her possessions and making hard choices. Downsizing her life because of need, not want.

"What else do you know about the family?" Emily asked, wanting to fill the silence to stop her thoughts spiralling. "How d'you meet them?"

Agnes moved closer to the kitchen, rubbing her eyes. "I haven't met them, not in person. The vet recommended I put an ad up on TradeMe and see if anyone responded. The Murchison's seemed the keenest of all the enquiries I got."

Emily nodded. TradeMe was the New Zealand equivalent of eBay or Craigslist. Although mostly used to sell second-hand goods, services or specialised goods could also be negotiated.

"Did you have a lot of responses?"

"A dozen emails on the first day and a few came through in the week following." Agnes sighed and clicked her fingers. Maude came running over to sit obediently by her side. "I like the idea of them having children for her to play with. And they had a really big back yard."

She glanced out the kitchen window at the small contained area at the back of her section. The house was part of a subdivided section where the original quarter acre now supported four houses with varying amounts of land.

From what Emily had seen from peering up the driveway, Agnes had the smallest parcel of the lot.

"It sounds ideal. I wonder if they'll let you visit when you're settled in your place."

Agnes gave a derisive snort. "Not likely. I'm shifting into the home because I can't take care of everything myself, anymore. They took my driver's license off me at the last test, and I doubt the buses will run very close."

Emily was about to suggest the family might bring Maude to visit her, then closed her mouth with the thought trapped on the inside of her lips. It wasn't her place to negotiate and to suggest such a thing might just bring hope where there was none.

"Did you finish up in the bedroom?" she asked instead. "Gregory's pretending very hard to be busy outside, but he's not. I can call him in if you still need a hand."

"No, I'm done. It's just all the old bedding in there now to be got rid of." Agnes shook her head. "I tried calling the Sallies about the bed since it's too big for your store, but they wouldn't take it."

"Yeah." Emily had heard the same report a few times, lately. "People just like to buy some things brand new."

Agnes clicked her tongue. "When I was a girl, you saved money where you could. I understand about the mattress"— she screwed her nose up—"that's just nasty, but I don't know what folks think they're going to catch off the frame. It's just wood."

"We're packed to go whenever you're ready," Gregory said as he walked inside. "I've loaded the boxes to go to the home, into the car."

"I might give the family a call," Agnes said, wetting her lips and glancing at her watch. "If they were just running late, I'd expect they'd have texted or phoned by now."

"Is that for Maude?" Gregory asked, patting his thighs to encourage the dog to jump up on him.

Emily winced. His jeans were dark indigo. Maude's white hairs would stand out like small beacons.

"There's somebody now," she said, hearing the unmistakable sound of a car slowing. She crossed into the lounge and lifted the net curtain. "It's a blue Kia Carnival."

"That'll be them." Agnes's voice sounded relieved but when Emily turned back, the sheen of tears was in her eyes.

She jerked her attention back to the road, not wanting to add to the lady's distress. "There's only the mother, by the looks of it."

The woman had got out of the car, the lock double beeping, but now just stood by the car. As a frown blossomed on Emily's face, the lady smoothed the front of her jeans and hooked her chestnut bob behind her right ear. After pulling her cream T-shirt down by the hem, she straightened her back and headed for the front door.

A twinge of unease curled in Emily's chest, moving up to tighten her throat as she turned to stare at Maude. The dog looked back at her sad eyes, the downturn of her mouth adding to the forlorn expression.

"Welcome," Agnes said from the entrance. "I was beginning to give up hope."

The woman answered. Something stiff and polite and so quiet Emily couldn't catch the words. Even Gregory appeared worried.

"But I can't—" Agnes said after a moment of the woman talking. "It's not possible. We had an agreement."

A minute later, and the woman returned to her car, adjusted the rear-view mirror and accelerated away.

Agnes walked into the lounge, wringing her hands together. "She told me her husband got a job opportunity up in Auckland and they can't possibly take the dog now."

Gregory winced and pulled his phone out of his pocket. Emily took a few steps toward Agnes, then Maude barrelled in front of her, leaping up on her mistress's legs with such force, she fell back a step.

"What am I going to do?" Agnes said in a plaintive wail. "The home won't allow her to stay and I don't know anybody else who'll take her. I can't have her put down!"

CHAPTER TWO

Already knowing she'd regret the decision, Emily stepped forward and tugged on Maude's collar until she fell back level. Agnes was in enough of a state without the added weight of her dog trying to throw her off balance.

"Don't you worry about a thing," Emily said in a firm voice. "I can look after Maude until we find a new family." She tried not to shiver as she imagined the reception this decision would have from her ghost cat.

"Can you really do that?"

"Of course." Emily gave Maude another pat, careful not to wipe her hand on her trouser leg afterwards. "There's enough room in my house for the two of us, and it won't be forever. I'm sure we'll find another family with children in no time flat."

Agnes gave a sob of relief and pressed her hand to her chest. "Thank goodness. I can't tell you how grateful I am. This day's hard enough without those wretched people changing their mind."

"Let's get into the car and take you over to the village

now, then," Emily said with a nod to Gregory. "Since we no longer need to wait around for someone to show."

A look of uncertainty crossed Agnes's face again, but she gave a nod. "Okay. Should we drop Maude off at your home first?"

"How about we take her along with us, so she knows you're okay in your new room? That way, if she's pining for you, I can bring her along for a visit without causing her further distress."

And I don't want to leave her alone in my house for the afternoon.

The journey to Stoneybrook Acres didn't take long. A discreet sign advertised the residence, complete with an elderly couple hand-in-hand, laughing. As they got out of the car, Emily stood on tiptoe. She could see her two-storey neighbour's house from there.

"I hope you're happy in charge of the boxes," she said to Gregory. "We'll go ahead and check-in or whatever it is you do here."

He seemed relieved to be left back at the car.

The front of the home sported a semi-circular driveway with a large oval garden in the centre. Burnished orange marigolds bobbed their heads in the mild easterly breeze, which cut through the heat of the day.

Most of the plants were dead-headed, having already displayed their finery and retired for another year. The soil of the beds was turned and composted, reminding Emily she should do the same to her own small patch of garden out the back.

The main building of the village was old brick while wings sprouted off in different directions, made of wood, modern brickettes with stylised discolouration, and plaster-board. Everywhere Emily turned, there seemed to be another part of the complex, all set within a woodland boundary.

No wonder she had no neighbours over the back fence —Stoneybrook Acres must own all that land.

As they approached the double doors of the entrance, a jackhammer started up from the side of the main building.

"I hope that doesn't carry on for too long," Agnes said with a worried glance in its direction. "I've got enough of a headache from packing up for the last week, without machinery banging on."

The receptionist must have overheard the concern because she offered up a large smile as the two women approached. "It's just due to a plumbing emergency," she reassured Agnes. "A burst pipe that happened to be right under the barbecue patio. We only just got the concrete poured for that late last year." She grimaced.

"What sort of plumbing?" Agnes's voice sounded anything but reassured. "Should I stay at home for another night to be safe?"

"There's no danger," the receptionist said. "It's just caused the water pressure to drop. Once they patch it up, you won't notice a thing."

"We're moving in a new resident." Emily cast a look at the woman's name badge. Margaret Tillerson. "If you could direct us to Agnes Myrtle's room, that would be great, Margaret."

Emily earned herself a scowl from the woman in question.

"I'm perfectly capable of talking for myself, thank you." Agnes lifted her nose into the air. "I might not be able to do everything, but rest assured my mouth still works."

"If you follow me," Margaret said, stopping any potential squabbles in their tracks. "I'll take you down to the room. And who's this?" she asked as she spotted Maude hiding behind Agnes's legs.

"This is Maude. Don't worry," Agnes hurried to say before the woman could protest, "she won't be staying. Emily is going to take her until we find her a new permanent home."

"What a looker you are, Maude." Margaret bent for a second, staring into the dog's eyes, then straightened up and walked at a slow pace down the hall. "You're on the east side of the building with a nice view out to the woodland."

It became clear as they travelled farther along the corridor, it also overlooked the burst pipe. The noise of the jackhammer increased until idle conversation was impossible. Emily clenched her teeth together to stop them vibrating in time with the machine's blows.

The room was small, a single bed along one wall opposite a table and chair. A recliner used up the far corner while a doorway led through to a small bathroom. The toilet, shower, and basin were in such proximity claustrophobia ate up the air in Emily's lungs. A wardrobe only a foot wide was behind the door while a television set was mounted on a bracket in the corner above it.

"Isn't this nice?" Margaret said, yelling to be heard above the noise from the garden.

Agnes cast a desultory glance around the compact space and nodded. "It's just like the one I was shown on my tour."

"The view is usually better," Margaret said, whipping the curtain to one side to uncover a man operating the jackhammer. His shorts had ridden down and Emily gave a guilty start at how much of the crack in his rear end she could see.

"Oh!" Margaret nearly tore the curtain in her haste to

pull it across the window again. "Perhaps, we're better off leaving that where it is for the time being."

Agnes wrinkled her nose and caught Emily's eye. The two of them burst into giggles at the exact same moment.

"If you need any help to get settled in, let me know." Margaret paused for a second, hand on her hip, then shook her head and retreated into the hallway. "The director of the home is up in Christchurch for the day at a conference, but I should be able to answer any questions you have."

"Thank you," Emily said, closing the door when it seemed Margaret might linger. When she turned to Agnes, she raised her eyebrows. "About that view."

The woman laughed and pulled the curtain back, fixing it with a tie at the side. "If the man wants to display what God gave him, I'm not going to put impediments in his path."

Maude nosed the door open into the bathroom, took a long glance around, then backed up and leapt for the bed. She didn't quite make it the first time, her forward legs hitting the spread just before gravity took her back to ground level. When she tried again, with Agnes's help this time, she made it. With her back legs splayed out to either side, she laid her head on her front paws.

"I'm not sure that's a look of approval," Agnes said, rubbing the dog along her backbone. "She's used to a much bigger space."

"It's a pity they don't let you have dogs here," Emily commented, glancing past the machine operator at the land-scaped forest running along the side. "There seems to be enough room out there for Maude to enjoy herself."

But that was the wrong thing to say and Agnes's lip wobbled. Emily excused herself, retreating out of the room on the excuse of chasing up Gregory.

The young man sat in the reception room, the two main boxes on either side of his chair. He rose at glacial speed when Emily walked into the room. "I wasn't sure if you wanted me to bowl on in there while she was getting settled."

"Good call." Emily waved him back into his seat and took the leather chair beside him. "It might be a good idea to give her a few minutes." She sighed and glanced around the space, feeling a slow sadness creeping up the back of her throat.

It'll be you, next.

"I think this place must take some getting used to." Gregory tapped his fingers in a dreamy rhythm on the arm of his chair. "No wonder they call it God's waiting room. I can't imagine how awful it would be to live here."

AFTER UNPACKING HER TREASURES, Agnes's room appeared lived-in but also a great deal smaller. Emily stood near the door, afraid to move in case she knocked something with her leg or elbow.

"I'll take these back out to the car." Gregory picked up the empty cardboard boxes and whistled as he walked out of the place.

Emily hovered in the doorway, unsure of how to leave without upsetting Agnes, not wanting to stay.

Maude solved that problem. She dismounted the bed with a huff of effort then belted out the door. Emily felt her brush by before her brain engaged enough to think to stop her. The dog was a few metres down the corridor before she turned and gave chase.

"Come back," she said in a loud whisper. Emily didn't

want to draw attention to the illegal dog being here by shouting. Unfortunately, Maude ignored the order and barrelled farther along the hall.

"Maude!" Agnes stood in the doorway, a frown creasing her forehead while a smile of pleasure danced across her lips. "Don't be a bad dog."

Emily reached out for the bulldog as she slowed, turning back towards her mistress's voice. Just as she snagged her collar, Maude took off again. Emily's fingers slipped on the leather and she gave a cry of frustration.

"What the—" another resident said, clutching at the neck of her dressing gown as Maude ran past her open door. "No dogs allowed."

"I'm sorry," Emily called out as she hobbled by. "We're trying to get her out of here."

Maude stopped at the corner, growling in the back of her throat at something or someone Emily couldn't see. She edged out to the side, trying to glance around the junction in the corridor while tensing herself to make another dive.

"Bad dog!" a sharp voice called out.

Maude whined and backed up a step, then recommenced her growl. The hairs on Emily's forearms raised, signalling their displeasure. She ignored her trepidation and snagged the dog's collar, this time holding it tight.

Around the bend, another dog sat on its haunches, eyeing Maude with a stern frown. The German Shepherd didn't appear to enjoy the sight of its English counterpart. Its silken brown eyes narrowed as Emily picked up the bulldog and cradled her close to her chest.

"No dogs allowed," the woman standing beside the other dog said. "Didn't you read the rule book before you came inside?"

Emily took a step back, affronted that someone so obviously breaking the rules herself had the temerity to quote them.

As if hearing her thoughts, the woman reached down to pat her dog on the head. "I've been granted permission, but the director would've told me if anyone else met the brief."

"We were just leaving," Emily said, giving Maude a last reassuring pat before restoring her back to the ground. "Her mummy moved in today and wanted to say one last goodbye."

The woman sniffed. "Doesn't she own a lead?"

"What brief did you meet to be allowed to keep your dog here?" Emily asked, ignoring the woman's impertinence to ask a pressing question of her own. "Are there a set of guidelines we could check?"

"The director will've talked over all of that with your —?" The woman stopped talking and raised her eyebrows.

"My friend."

Emily was about to press for a better answer when the German Shepherd gave a large bark and took off at a sprint along the corridor. Maude struggled free of Emily's grip to give chase.

"Conker! Come back here at once," the woman shouted.

To Emily's delight, the dog ignored the command. If anything, his race down the hallway grew more enthusiastic. The two dogs disappeared around the corner, into the reception room. Agnes shuffled along the hallway, having switched direction when Maude ran past her.

"Your dog must have done something to upset Conker," the woman said with such utter certainty that Emily found herself nodding along with the preposterous idea. Rather than stay and argue the toss, she followed in Maude's footsteps, giving Agnes a wink as she passed.

"Oh, no," she said as the dogs used the opportunity presented by a new arrival to slip out the entrance doors.

A man in a dark grey suit stood there, nonplussed, as the two animals raced past him. "We don't allow dogs," he said in a confused voice and Emily laughed as she passed by him.

"It appears someone relaxed the policy," she called out in a merry tone, before chasing the dogs outside, into the retirement home grounds.

MAUDE GAVE up the game well before Conker. The German Shepherd was furiously barking at the man operating the jackhammer, while the bulldog had stopped a few metres away from the entrance, choosing to collapse in the shade of a gigantic oak tree.

"Good dog," Emily cooed as she approached, although the dog hadn't been anything of the sort. "Don't start running again, okay. My knees are already yelling."

Your dogs are barking her mind helpfully provided, the thought earning a smile.

It seemed Maude agreed with her as she let Emily grab hold of her collar without any further attempt to run away. She gave a small bark, of welcome more than in warning. The other dog echoed her, not settling for just one.

"That woman in the hall was right," Emily said to the dog, keeping her voice nice and light—a memory from someone who'd gone through dog-training. The advice had stuck though she couldn't for the life of her remember where it originated. "I should have you on a lead."

She cast her eye around, as though there'd be a handy piece of leather to snap onto the dog's collar lying nearby.

The trunk of the oak caught her eye. Not because there was anything useful to hand but for the network of deep wounds entwining the base of the tree.

It appeared someone or something had injured it badly when it was smaller. Now, the bark swelled out like balloons on either side of the cut, while bare wood still winked out, the lighter colour reminiscent of old bones.

Fresher marks, similar in nature, were scored further up the trunk. An attacker coming back much later for another go.

But that wasn't finding her a leash.

"You'll just have to put up with me dragging you," Emily said after a few minutes. "And if you try that again, I'll lock you in the car alone."

A dire warning sounded in her head at that speech. *Don't leave your dog in a hot car.* Even saying it as a joke to the dog felt wrong.

Speaking of the car, Gregory lounged nearby the vehicle, his attention once again glued to his phone. If she wasn't handling the dog, Emily might have texted him a message to come inside the home. Not because she needed him for anything but just for the reluctance that would cross his face.

"Don't bring the dog back inside," the grey-suited man said as Emily walked Maude through the entrance. "He shouldn't be here."

"There was another dog roaming the premises who started the trouble," Emily said, ignoring him the same way she ignored the nagging pain in her hip. "If you allow one, it's hypocritical to deny another."

Agnes waited anxiously near the reception counter and took a few tentative steps towards her dog, her hands once again clenched together. "Maude was just visiting to see where I lived," she said in an apologetic tone.

"What are the requirements to let a dog live with a resident?" Emily straightened up as she sent Maude on her way over to Agnes. "I don't believe you let Ms Myrtle know there was an option to keep her pet."

The woman from the corridor came to greet them, her cheeks flushed with blood. "I told her," she said to the man. "I said this bulldog wouldn't meet the conditions. She brought that dog in here without any regard to the rules."

"Mrs Wilberforce's dog is a therapy animal." The man spoke slowly and enunciated every word with care.

Emily felt the heat rising, warming the skin of her neck before rushing up to colour her cheeks. He thought she was feeble-minded, that's what the pedantic tones told her. "So is Maude." She put her hands on her hips, glaring. "What right do you have to turn down her placement here?"

"My name is Allain Homeaway and I'm the director of operations for Stoneybrook Acres. I make the rules and apply them, that's what rights I have."

"If you have experience, then it should be patently obvious that Maude can be nothing but good for Ms Myrtle. Just look at them."

She pointed, but Allain didn't even turn his head to follow her direction. "There are guidelines. The dog must be licensed as a therapy animal before we can even consider such a thing."

Mrs Wilberforce's gaze jerked away from the conversation and she stared intently at a rubber plant in the corner, her hands lacing together. Emily narrowed her eyes as she assessed the woman quickly. Her cheeks had already been flushed but now a bright blush stained all the way down to the top button in her blouse.

Emily had always been a blusher. She knew exactly what the rush of colour meant. "Conker isn't a therapy animal."

She addressed the words to Allain but kept her eyes fixed on Mrs Wilberforce. Oh, yes. She'd hit the nail on the head. The woman's eyes now ping-ponged around the room in nervous glances, left and right.

Shifty. That's how she looked.

"If Conker was approved without the official documentation, then you should extend the same courtesy to Maude. I'm certain that Agnes's doctor will attest to the necessity of keeping her beloved animal close to her side."

"I can assure you that Mrs Wilberforce's dog passed all—"

"He's a cadaver dog," Mrs Wilberforce suddenly yelled.

Allain shot a concerned glance in her direction, then shook his head and returned his attention to Emily. "As I was saying—"

"No! You don't understand." Mrs Wilberforce ran forward a few steps, tugging on Allain's sleeve and pointing towards the entrance door. Her face had drained of its blushes. Now her skin was pale and cold. "He used to work for the police until he retired. Conker is a *cadaver* dog!"

Emily traced the invisible line where Mrs Wilberforce's finger pointed and felt her heart drop down into her stomach.

Conker sat outside the entrance door, ears pricked up in an alert stance.

At his feet was a large bone.

gnes held back, cuddling Maude close as Emily followed the director out the front door and around the side of the building. Gregory kept pace with her, finally discovering an interest that sped him up to normal.

"Keep back," Allain yelled as he spotted the jack-hammer operator—the machine now blessedly silent—picking out chunks of concrete from the barbeque area.

For a second, Emily thought he was yelling at the man, but Allain turned and with a large arm-gesture waved them back.

"Sod that for a joke," Gregory said, continuing onward, and Emily smiled as she walked briskly by his side.

"Call the police," the machine operator called out as they approached. His face was ruddy with heat and his hair dripped with sweat. When he shook his head, a fine spray of droplets flew out to either side. "There's somebody buried here."

"Let me see," Allain insisted, crowding the man until he stepped back, a piece of chipped concrete in his hands. "Why, this could be anything. The body of a pet or a wild animal or a... a..." He turned back to where Conker sat, on alert, at the corner of the retirement home complex. "Or a dog!"

"It's not a dog, mate." The jackhammer operator wiped his gloved hand over his forehead, soaking up the sweat but leaving behind a streak of grease and dirt. His eyes moved from Allain to Emily, then Gregory. "It's a body. A human body."

"You've got your phone, don't you?" Emily turned to Gregory. "Can you give the police station a call?"

"Do I use the emergency number?" Gregory looked worried as he fiddled the device out of his jeans' pocket.

"I wouldn't." Emily's eyes glanced back toward the entrance and she gave a shudder. "The bones look to have been buried for quite a while. Use the local number, that'll be best. Sergeant Winchester should be in the office."

While he followed her instructions, Emily walked closer to the demolished patio. She caught a flash of white and light brown in the corner of the hole, then turned to the man still holding a piece of concrete in his hand. "Did you find the burst pipe yet?"

The man shook his head, his eyes returning to the dark pit in the ground while his free hand tugged at the collar of his hi-vis jacket. "I know where the leak is, but I'll need more time to get to it." He waved a hand at the excavation. "It's under that."

"Then I guess your work is done here for the day," Emily said, touching him lightly on the arm when the man's eyes wandered away. "I can't imagine the police will allow you to continue."

He nodded, glancing over at Allain with a frown, then swallowing hard while his eyes crept back to the grave. "I'll pack up the tools, then, and get them out of everybody's way."

"The sergeant's on his way," Gregory said, slipping his phone back into the front pocket. "He said not to touch anything in the meantime."

With one hand on the jackhammer, the worker stopped and sighed. "I guess that means me, too," he said in a resigned tone.

"It means all of us," Emily said, her voice firm. "I think it's time we headed back inside."

WHILE THE POLICE examined the scene, Emily hovered indoors, anxiously checking on their progress through the window. Although there was a relatively large group gathered in the reception area, they were all quiet. Even the dogs picked up on the tone, staying by their mistress's sides with their mouths shut.

"Okay," Sergeant Winchester said as he walked through the entrance doors. "Which one of you is in charge of this place?"

Allain stepped forward, his formerly haughty expression now coated with a thin layer of fear. "That'll be me, officer. Can you tell me what's happening out there?"

"What's happening is that there's a dead body and we need to find out the identity. Do you have any patients missing?"

"Residents," Allain said with a frown. "This is a retirement community, not a hospital."

"You do have hospital facilities in here, don't you?"

The director nodded. "For some of our residents it's a

necessity but for most of our elderly guests, this is their home."

The sergeant nodded, his gaze flicking back over his shoulder as a young constable appeared. "Did you secure the area?"

Emily recognised the younger man as one who'd laughed at her in a prior encounter. She'd tried to report a murder a few months before and he'd thought it a great joke. PC Perry, if she wasn't mistaken. The memory of the event still rankled.

The officer nodded. "It's all taped off and we're just waiting for the pathologist to finish up examining the bones."

"And?" The sergeant raised his eyebrows.

PC Perry stared back at him, his lips twisting. "Sorry?"

"And why did you come in to tell me this? Don't you think your time would be better spent out there, searching for evidence?"

The young man stared at the floor, a crimson stain rising above the collar of his light-blue shirt. "The pathologist asked me to collect the original bone."

"Go, fetch," Emily said under her breath, earning a chuckle from Gregory.

"It's behind the reception desk," Allain said, moving over to the counter. "We thought it best to move it out of the way. We don't want any more of our residents to know about this than already do."

The sergeant nodded at Perry, who scuttled around behind the desk.

"You'll have a hard time keeping a lid on this," Winchester said to the director. "It's not something we'll be able to clear up in an afternoon."

"Sure, sure," Allain said, most of his attention fixed on PC Perry as he lifted the bone between two fingers.

"Gloves!" the sergeant barked, and the younger man dropped the bone, the stain now moving from his collar up to his cheeks.

"I'll need to have a word with the worker digging up the concrete," the sergeant said, his gaze immediately going to the hi-vis vested worker. "If you're free now, we can do this here. Otherwise, I'll take your name and address and we can meet you down at the station."

"Here, please," the worker hurried to answer. "The sooner the better. I've got jobs piling up while we're just standing here."

"Fine." Sergeant Winchester returned his stern gaze to Allain. "Do you have a suitable room I can commandeer for the remainder of the afternoon?"

As soon as Emily, Gregory, and Agnes had given their names to the police, they decamped from the reception area back to Agnes's small room. "We should probably get back to work," Emily said, then sat down on the edge of the bed.

"You can see everything from here," Gregory said with an approving note in his voice. He walked to the window and drew the drapes back even further as he cast his gaze around the garden. "Oh!"

"See a bit much, did you?" Agnes asked as the young man took a sudden step back.

"There was a skull." Gregory crossed his arms over his chest. "Perhaps I don't need to watch as much as I thought I did."

The two women laughed and nodded. "Although," Agnes added, "I daresay it'll be the most entertaining thing to happen around here."

"There's the bingo every Friday, remember?" Emily said with a grin. "And I'm not sure this counts as entertainment."

"I just hope it's not one of the previous residents." Agnes pulled a face. "Could you imagine if it turns out to be somebody from here?"

"I don't know who else it would be." Gregory's brow furrowed. "It doesn't seem a likely place for someone to choose as a burial site if the body isn't from this place."

"Not if it's recent," Emily agreed. "For body disposal, being in full view of an entire rest home doesn't strike me as a good choice. The bones might be older than this place though."

"They'd have to be really old in that case," Agnes said. "I think this building has been here for a long time, at least dating back to the forties. Before it was a retirement village, it was a school or an orphanage—something like that—and dad said they used it for recuperating soldiers after the war."

Emily leaned her head to one side as she thought. "If it was a hospital after the war, then it might have a burial ground on site for those soldiers who didn't make it. I think a lot of older places had that sort of arrangement. Especially if they didn't have family nearby."

Gregory frowned and his gaze flickered to the window again before he forced his eyes to the floor. "I don't know much about bones and skeletons, but it didn't strike me as old as all that."

Unfortunately, Emily knew what he meant. It mightn't have been a full arm or leg that Conker had dragged up to the door but, for a skeleton, it had been chunky.

As the thought entered her head, her stomach protested. "How about we talk about something pleasant instead? Do you think the director will change his mind about Maude?"

"I think he's forgotten all about her," Agnes said with a

twinkle in her eye. "If you could fetch me the box of her supplies that I put into the boot, I might move her in here while his attention is distracted elsewhere."

"It's certainly worth a shot," Emily agreed, giving Gregory a nod to go and retrieve Maude's belongings. She felt a sense of satisfaction that she didn't have to explain a new arrival to Peanut. Her ghost cat might not have a lot of physical presence, but he still acted as though her entire house belonged to him.

"Sergeant Winchester asked for you to go see him," Gregory said on his return. Maude jumped up on his leg, sniffing with excited determination at the base of the box.

"Me?" Emily stood up from the bed, her heart beginning to thump harder. "What for?"

"He asked me a couple of questions about when the dogs were running about. I imagine it's more of the same."

"Don't worry," Agnes said with a cheeky smile. "If you give us the signal, we'll rescue you from the po-po."

Gregory burst out laughing, his eyes widening in surprise. "You're down with the lingo, huh? What else do you old folks talk about on the street?"

Emily straightened her blouse as she walked to the reception area. The day's events jumbled in her mind and her tongue felt swollen. Her encounters with police had been few and far between. She was more familiar with the officers in her favourite TV shows than the few she'd met in real life.

Margaret raised her eyebrows, leaning her body on the counter as Emily approached.

"I was told the sergeant wanted to see me?"

"He's in Allain's office," Margaret said, pointing to a door off the main room. "Don't worry about the door being shut, there's no one else in there."

"Have you talked to him?"

"Yeah." She pursed her lips and scanned Emily. "Don't worry about it. He'll just ask some easy questions."

Emily nodded and walked over, rapping a knuckle on the door and waiting for a response before she entered.

"Close the door behind you," Sergeant Winchester said with a grim expression. "We don't need everyone around here listening in."

"I don't really know very much about—"

Emily broke off as the sergeant raised his hand. "How about you let me ask the questions I need answers to before you say anything else?"

"Fair enough." Emily sat in the chair opposite him and crossed her hands in her lap. The image of PCs Perry and Mitchell laughing leapt into her mind and she blinked them away.

"What time did you arrive at Stoneybrook?"

"I'm not sure." Emily glanced at her watch, an old habit but useless now because she couldn't read the digital numbers. "I've got a talking watch, but I set it to silent because we were helping Ms Myrtle to pack and move today."

"Just an approximation is fine."

Emily shrugged, as upset by her own nervousness as she was anxious about giving the right answer to the question. "Maybe two? It was after lunch, that's all I'm sure about."

"And why are you here?"

"As I said, we're here to help Agnes with her move."

The sergeant nodded and flicked back a few pages in his notebook. "When I spoke to Suzanne, she said you were the one handling the bulldog."

"Who?"

"Suzanne Wilberforce. The owner of the dog that found the bones."

Emily swallowed hard and nodded. "I bumped into her in the corridor. We brought Maude—the English bulldog—along with us because the family meant to be adopting her pulled out at the last minute. She was fine at first, then ran out of the room. I presume because she heard or smelled the other dog."

"They were outside together?"

"They both ran outside, but Maude didn't go near the —" Emily broke off, frowning.

"The crime scene?" Sergeant Winchester prompted.

"Yeah, there. She stopped just outside the entrance, by the large oak near the driveway. The German Shepherd kept running and when I went outside, he was barking at the jackhammer guy."

"So, you didn't get close to the remains?"

Emily nodded, then shrugged. "I did go outside again when Mrs Wilberforce explained her dog's old job. We didn't stand near the grave though. Not really. We just talked to the machine operator, then, when Gregory said you'd told everyone to leave stuff where it was, we came back inside."

The sergeant nodded and closed his notebook, folding his hands together on top. "Did you see anything else?"

Emily stared hard at the edge of the desk. "Just the broken-up concrete and a hole. Nothing really."

"No. I didn't mean that, I meant"—the sergeant cleared his throat—"did *you* notice something in particular."

When she just stared at him, not understanding the distinction, he sighed and ran a hand through his hair.

"Did you see any ghosts?"

Emily clamped her lips into a thin line. After the reception she'd received from the police the last time she mentioned spirits, this wasn't a question she'd expected to hear. She eyed the sergeant through narrowed lids, trying to spot the signs he was laughing at her expense.

Apart from shifting in his seat, the sergeant appeared normal.

"I didn't see anything, ghost or otherwise," Emily repeated. "If there's nothing more, I'd quite like to leave now. I still have things to pack up from Ms Myrtle's house to take back to work."

"Of course." Winchester nodded with such enthusiasm his fringe fell forward over his eyes. "You can go. Please let Ms Myrtle know that I'd like to see her next."

Emily exhaled slowly as she walked out of the office, closing the door firmly behind her. She gave a nod to Margaret, then shuffled down the corridor. After giving chase to Maude earlier, her hips and knees had stiffened.

"No handcuffs," she announced with a forced smile, walking back into Agnes's room. "But they want to see you next. We'll hang out with Maude until you get back, then the sergeant said we're free to go."

Agnes's interview took even less time than Emily's, and soon she and Gregory were outside, getting into the car.

Emily couldn't resist one more peek at the gravesite, but between the police officers, and the flapping yellow warning tape, she could see even less than before.

The one thing she certainly didn't see was a ghost.

CHAPTER FOUR

When Emily finished doing her leg stretches that night, she settled down onto the sofa with a large, grilled cheese sandwich and pulled her laptop close. Peanut crawled back and forth over her a few times, then curled up in her lap.

The stretching exercises were meant to keep her limbs limber, though, with each passing month, she lost flexibility. The neuropathy caused by her car accident meant her nerves didn't pass messages effectively to her muscles. On top of the illiteracy caused by damage to her language processing centre, the news had come as a nasty blow.

After visiting the facility she would most likely end up living within soon, Emily hadn't come away with a great impression. Still, it wouldn't be every day a corpse was dug up on their land. Once she deducted the anxiety that discovery had caused, the retirement home didn't seem quite as bad.

In between bites of her sandwich—with a full diced tomato added in to ease some of her guilt at the treat—Emily spoke a command for the computer to search the history of the Stoneybrook Acres property.

The first few pages were full of ads for the facility, or infomercial dumps meant to resemble first-hand accounts. Once she scrolled past those items, dismissing them as soon as the computer read out the headlines, Emily uncovered some meatier stuff.

As Agnes had suggested, the original building dated back to the thirties. A guest house set to accommodate visitors to Pinetar Beach, its initial construction held a lot more in common with a military barracks than an upscale resort.

When the war came, and the tourists departed, the building had converted into a training facility, requisitioned by the ministry of defence. The conversion into a respite hospital for wounded soldiers came later when the facilities in nearby Christchurch overflowed.

Emily smiled at one of the pictures from the era. A room—maybe even the same one housing Agnes—held two cots, side by side. Grinning soldiers in striped pyjamas waved to the camera. One had their leg in a sling while the other was missing most of one arm.

The injuries didn't phase them, not when it got them away from the front line.

Later photographs showed the minimal changes made to turn the complex into a reform school. Children, some as young as ten, were lined up in a photograph taken before the main entrance. They were boarded at the facility—males at the front of the building and females at the back. Too naughty to stay with their parents but not criminal enough to qualify for a true borstal.

The sight of children so young being forced into a school away from their parents and siblings filled Emily with sorrow. Some 'crimes' listed in the archives were so petty she couldn't imagine why it had upset folks enough to go to such extremes.

One child, aged twelve, had been boarded at the school for four years after stealing a bag of lolly mix from a local dairy. Another had thrown stones at cars passing on the main road in front of his house.

Naughty deeds, sure, but understandable. To receive something akin to a prison sentence for the mischief was the true crime in Emily's eyes.

Still, generations passed and what was considered acceptable changed along with the times. Perhaps, if she'd been raised in the same era, Emily would be horrified now that children could get away with so much.

In the seventies, the complex had changed hands again. This time, it altered into a retirement home with hospital facilities. Over the years since, as the general population aged while also living longer, Stoneybrook had expanded out in all directions.

Emily listened to the details of the current business. It held eighteen land parcels around the town of Pinetar, in addition to the main facility. They were separated by existing housing or businesses, her home one of the sites.

She supposed that as the existing properties came up for sale, the retirement facility would bid for the land until they could join the dots and expand. Until then, it was a safe purchase. House and land prices in New Zealand continued to be an investment almost guaranteed a good return.

As Peanut grew restless, demanding more attention, Emily closed the laptop and placed it on the floor. She lay on the sofa, stroking the back of her ghost cat until he purred in ecstasy.

Given that the last change to Stoneybrook took place

decades before, it made it most likely the body was related to the current business.

"I hope it was an accident," Emily whispered to the cat, who laid back his ears and paid full attention. "I'd much rather they find out a drunk fell in a hole and accidentally had concrete poured over him than find out somebody hid a body there on purpose."

For a body to be found under a patio didn't offer many explanations outside of wrongdoing, but she could still hold out hope. After being heavily involved in the last murder to take place in Pinetar, Emily had no wish to become entangled—even peripherally—in another one.

With the hour growing so late that even Peanut yawned, Emily switched the comforts of the sofa for the softness of her bed. The moon was a tiny sliver in the sky, barely casting any light, but the street lamps along the street made up for the lack.

She lay back, thinking of the bones and who they might belong to. As her mind wandered into a dream and out again, her ideas of how they might have got into the retirement home garden became ever stranger.

Emily drifted off to sleep, skeletons forming and dissolving before her eyes. Just as she embarked on a dream adventure, a hideous cry pulled her straight back out of sleep.

"Who the hell is that?" the ghost of Cynthia Pettigrew cried, pointing across the bedroom at a man, his shoulders hunched, his face wrinkled with age.

"Forget who he is, what are you doing here?" Emily sat up in bed, clutching the sheets to her chest and experiencing a strong sense of deja vu as the ghost glared at the new arrival.

"I pop back sometimes," Cynthia admitted. "Just to check on Peanut and see things are still ticking along okay."

Peanut ran over to his old mistress, his motor revving into a loud purr as she stroked his back and pulled his tail.

"Anyway, I'm allowed to visit. What I want to know is where you found your new friend?"

The male ghost didn't seem upset the two were discussing him without involving him in the conversation. He wavered back and forth on his feet, reminding Emily of herself when she grew tired.

"Hello," she said, pulling the bedclothes back and dragging her dressing gown up off the floor. "Who are you?"

The ghost didn't answer, just kept staring at Emily as though he'd never seen a woman before. It made her uncomfortable enough to double knot her robe.

"Don't be so rude," Cynthia said, causing Emily to burst into laughter. She was one to talk! The ghost was the rudest woman she'd ever met, and she'd faced down some stiff competition.

"Are you from Stoneybrook Acres?" Emily tried—an easy guess. "Did we uncover your bones?"

The man still didn't answer, though his attention turned toward the window, a change that Emily greeted with a sigh of relief.

"Hey, you." Cynthia snapped her fingers. "We're talking to you and the least you can do is answer."

Still no response. Emily felt the drag of tiredness hit her. Too much happening with too little sleep.

"Well, if you're not going to talk, would you at least do me the courtesy of going through to my lounge and waiting there till morning? No offence, but it's bad enough having this one"—she gestured at Cynthia—"paying me a visit at night. Having a man staring at me while I'm asleep is just a bit too creepy."

Peanut wandered closer to the new ghost, patting the man's foot with his paw.

"Mm," he said, the first sound he appeared to have uttered for a long time considering the croak. He whistled a short tune and Peanut stared up at him in wonder.

"Stop courting my cat." Cynthia had her hands on her hips and now tilted her head to one side. "I really do think you owe us some information before you start playing with our pet."

"I'm guessing that you two don't hang out together in ghost land, then." Emily moved toward the door, silencing a yawn with the back of her hand. If her night was going to be interrupted so rudely, the least she could do was make herself the treat of a hot drink.

"No," Cynthia said, following Emily into the kitchen. "I have better things to do with my time than hang around with a mute."

"I do wish you ghosts would choose a better time and place to appear than in my bedroom in the middle of the night."

"It's hardly midnight, dear." Cynthia gave a sniff and bent to pick up Peanut. The cat eyed the kitchen bench with enthusiasm, though it had been a long time since he'd been able to eat. "These days, you can barely make it to nine o'clock."

"How long have you been keeping tabs on me?"

Emily felt out of sorts and not just due to the interruption. Since she'd helped Cynthia track down her killer, she'd thought the ghost had moved onto a better place. To find out now that she'd hung around the whole time, just staying out of sight, made her feel violated.

"Just once in a while," the ghost said vaguely, leaning forward to rub her nose into Peanut's fur.

"For goodness' sake," Emily said, annoyed. "He's not a handkerchief!"

"I just like the way he smells. It reminds me of the good times from being alive."

"You've never told me about any good times," Emily said with a sniff. "From what I remember, you complained constantly about how terrible everyone and everything was."

"Well, perhaps you weren't paying attention. That's part and parcel of having a brain injury, isn't it?"

As she spooned out a few naughty sugars on top of her Chai tea bag, Emily suppressed a smile. Although loathe to admit it, she'd missed the verbal sparring of her old companion.

"Here he comes," Cynthia said as the male ghost shuffled into the room. "Full of energy and laughter, aren't you, chum?"

The ghost hovered in the passage between the kitchen and the lounge. Not wanting to walk straight through him, and sure asking him to move would be met with the same vacant stare, Emily drank her cup of chai in the kitchen, standing up. Not her favourite position to do anything.

"What are we going to do with you?" she asked as she rinsed out the mug. "If you can't communicate, then I'm not sure I'll be of any help."

"Why don't you call on Crystal Dreaming, then?" Cynthia said with a snide smile. "I'm sure she'll have an endless bounty of ideas."

"Don't be rude about my business partner." Emily stacked her cup in the dishwasher before covering her face with both hands. "And, yes, she might have some clue of what to try."

Crystal Dreaming was Pinetar's premium psychic. She couldn't actually communicate with the dead—at least so far as Emily could fathom—but she had great instincts, great insight, and a great customer base that the true ghost-seer had been glad to share.

Even though Emily didn't have control over which spirits visited her, she'd had some limited success with helping out frustrated townsfolk with their persistent ghosts.

Well, if a person's idea of limited was twice.

"Unless you have a better idea," Emily said, passing the buck straight back to Cynthia.

"You took me to my grave. It didn't help me out any, but perhaps that's worth another try?"

Emily glanced at the frail elderly gentleman. Yes. She was sure he belonged to the bones found earlier at Stoney-brook. She gave a long sigh before nodding. The idea was worth a go.

CHAPTER FIVE

The streetlamps outside Stoneybrook Acres didn't cast their light far into the retirement home grounds. But their meagre light would have to do since Emily refused to drive her car up to the door. It was bad enough to have Cynthia yapping in her ear. She didn't want anyone else to find her in the grounds of an illegal burial site at night.

By the third time she tripped over some unknown object in the dark, she'd changed her mind. A pity it was too late by then.

"Keep up," Cynthia snapped, floating over the uneven ground without a care in the world. She'd been reluctant to leave Peanut back at home but finally did at Emily's behest. It appeared she intended to take that out on her at every step.

The male ghost trailed along behind. He might not be able to talk or express himself in any way, but he seemed happy enough to follow.

"It's quite nice, you know," Cynthia said. "Having a man stay silent for so long. When I was alive, it felt like one was always in my face, mansplaining something incorrectly."

That tickled Emily's funny bone, and she held the smile until her foot hit against a tree root or a rock and she stumbled, placing far too much weight on her sore hip. The jolt of pain slammed into her like a dagger, causing tears of pain to spring into her eyes.

"Careful," Cynthia said.

Emily turned, ready with a retort, then saw her friend was gesturing to the flapping police tape. She'd almost walked straight into it.

"Hey, mister," Emily whispered to the male ghost. "Do you recognise anything around here?"

He stopped walking forward, but that was his only response.

"Boy, this is a creepy place at night, isn't it?" Cynthia moved closer to Emily, her eyes darting around the large building. During the day it had sprawled but, in the darkness, it hunched down like a large animal ready to pounce.

"It gets worse when you consider this poor bloke's grave is just a few metres away." Emily couldn't see the outline of the hole in the gloom but could feel it as a physical presence. The draw of death and destruction were palpable in the night.

"There aren't that many things I'm grateful for about dying young, but not ending up in a cage like this is one of them."

Emily shot Cynthia a sharp look that she probably couldn't see. "They're not cages. The rooms are very nice, although a bit on the small side."

"Boxes, then. Does that make it better?"

Emily's gaze moved to Agnes's window, just a glint of reflected moonlight to distinguish it from the old brickwork.

No, it didn't make it better. The fear of ending up in this place, or one like it, crawled up the back of her throat.

"Imagine if they'd put a nice hotel here, instead," Cynthia mused. "Wouldn't that be so much better than this awful place?"

"It was a hotel of sorts." Emily grinned as she thought of the disappointed expressions on the faces of any tourists unlucky enough to book a room here. "Just not a successful one, from what I can tell."

"No kidding." Cynthia floated farther along the lawn, angling toward the dense blackness of the wooded edge. "I remember the trouble I had with Nathaniel's house, it being so old. The first six months after I moved in, we had construction crews there every day trying to turn it from a damp brick box into something light and liveable."

Emily took her shoes off and followed behind Cynthia, letting her toes sink into the damp earth. The grass was much kinder to her feet than the tight leather of her mules. Even the most sensible footwear had nothing on a nicely kept lawn.

"What's your man doing now?" Cynthia asked, pointing back toward the taped off section.

He was shuffling forward, past the hole where his own remains were buried—or might even be excavated by now— and straight through the yellow tape barrier on the other side.

About three windows down from Agnes's room, the ghost stopped and bent to place his hands flat on the ground. He whistled a short tune. Even though he didn't say the words, Emily heard the echo of a thousand children's games in her mind. *Olly olly oxen free.*

The whistle was so discordant with their current location that Emily's scalp prickled. She ran a hand through her curls, itching the skin beneath gently with her nails. She didn't want to release a drift of dandruff snowflakes.

Cynthia shook her head, her upper lip curling. "You really lucked into a mental case with this one, didn't you?"

"It seems to be the pattern," Emily agreed, enjoying the slight gasp her friend made as the ramification set in.

"Hey, mister," Cynthia called out. "Do you mind working out who you are a bit quicker so we can get out of here and go someplace nice? You're getting boring."

"Getting?" Emily raised an eyebrow. "That's generous of you."

"I'm not a harridan all the time." Cynthia sniffed. "Just a lot of it. How's Peanut doing?"

The change in subject took Emily a second to catch up with. "Okay." She frowned. "Although, from what you said before, you've been checking up on him yourself. The next time you visit, please wake me."

"I was being kind, Scarface. It's obvious you need your rest."

"It's not restful, knowing that somebody comes and stares at me while I'm asleep. I'd rather stay awake while you're in the house, and doze late the next morning."

Cynthia gave a snort of amusement. "I wasn't the one staring. It's your new boyfriend who was doing that."

Emily's mouth pulled down at the corners. "Really? I could've done without knowing that tidbit of information."

"You'll know it soon enough if he can't tell us who he is," Cynthia pointed out. "It was hard enough finding out who killed me so I could move on. With mute man, it'll be a miracle if he finds the light."

"What's on the other side of the light?" Emily tried not to glance in Cynthia's direction. She really didn't want the ghost to see how much she craved knowing the truth.

"None of your business. You'll find it all out soon enough."

"Not even a hint?"

"Don't be so maudlin." Cynthia walked away, making a beeline for the male ghost. "You want to concentrate your attention on making this life the best it can be, not worrying about the next one."

She tapped the man on the shoulder. He glanced up but just stared blankly at her for a while before returning his attention to the ground. He repeated the whistle again.

Cynthia shuddered. "I really wish you wouldn't do that, pal. You don't know who'll take advantage."

Emily was glad she wasn't the only one freaked out, but not as glad as she would be to leave this cursed place and go home. "How about we head back to the car and see if he'll follow? This isn't doing anything to help."

"Let me guess," Cynthia said, turning. "The next step in your grand plan is to call the town medium. Maybe she can move him along."

"Don't snipe about Crystal," Emily said as she headed for the driveway. "It's not her fault she can't talk to you."

"I'm not upset she doesn't speak to me, it's a blessing."

"Tag!"

The strange voice caught Emily's attention, and she jerked around. The tone was young, but she couldn't see a source except for the male ghost. "Who was that?" she called out, forgetting to whisper.

"You're it!"

Another voice. Again, it sounded young but different from the previous call.

"Hey, mate," Cynthia called out. "How about you knock that off, okay?"

Emily noticed how she cupped her elbows. A scared

ghost did nothing to ease her own nerves.

The male ghost stood up, shaking his legs out and cracking his neck from side to side. He whistled for the third time.

"Stuff this for a joke," Cynthia declared, drifting farther away. "If I wanted an episode of the Twilight Zone, I'd stay indoors and watch the telly."

A child's laugh rang out, echoing off the side of the retirement home and bouncing back toward Emily. By now, her gut was churning. Her scalp no longer prickled, it was a swarm of beestings, her hair standing on end.

"Can I play?"

As Emily's throat tightened to a thin straw, a hand popped up through the manicured lawn past the barbeque patio. A child's hand.

It felt around in a circle, then pressed its palm flat on the grass, hauling a ghost body out of the ground. The child, or young teenager, got his upper body out, then leaned on his arms for better leverage.

"Oh, my." Cynthia's voice was full of distress. "Who's your friend?"

Another hand poked up through the grass, this time the child ghost grabbed hold to pull his companion free of the earth. The two boys stared at each other, then broke into giggles. Their laughter grew and grew until they had to clasp each other by the shoulders to stand.

Emily wanted to run home. She didn't care about her decaying muscles or the pain in her hip. As a third hand sprang up from the soil, her lungs felt as though they were being squeezed too tightly to draw breath.

"How many more do you have stored down there?" Cynthia asked the male ghost, her voice streaking into the upper registers. "A whole classroom?"

But the man continued to ignore her. His eyes flicked from one young boy to another, a smile of contentment on his pale face.

"Hey, how about we call it a night?" It took all of Emily's courage, but she forced herself to take a step forward. The second was harder, her feet stuck in cement blocks buried thigh-deep in quicksand. "We can visit again in the morning."

The morning. With daylight. Where each new apparition wouldn't stun her with fear.

"That's a great idea," Cynthia said in her new, high voice. "These boys look as though they need a good rest."

With the way they ran around each other, calling and laughing, it seemed the opposite was true. The man stood in the centre of them, a feature of their game. He spun, tracking the boys as they tagged and wrestled, slapped and tickled.

Emily closed her eyes, the sight too exhausting to keep bearing witness. "Old ghost man, can you ask your new friends for their names?"

Another set of giggles rippled through the young teens, rewarding her with smiles of delight rather than an answer.

"What on earth do you think you're doing out here at this time of night?" a man's voice asked from behind Emily.

With a shimmer, the boys disappeared, melting into the ground like snowmen under a summer sun.

Emily turned, the new spike of fear returning the gift of movement. PC Perry stood with his feet wide apart, one hand on his belt and the other on the handle of his baton.

"This is an active crime scene," he said with a scowl. "If you don't give me a good excuse for being here, I'm dragging you down to the station right now."

CHAPTER SIX

"I just want to talk to the sergeant," Emily repeated for the fifth time. "I understand he's not in the station now, but I'm happy to go home and come back when he is." She yawned, showing the reason she preferred that option.

Except it wasn't a choice on offer. PC Perry fixed her with the same glare he'd bestowed on her since finding her in the Stoneybrook grounds. Truth be told, it was wearing a bit thin.

"Until you tell me what you were doing, I'm not releasing you."

"But you said I wasn't under arrest," Emily said, tapping her finger on the table. "If I'm free to go, then that's what I want to do."

"You're not under arrest, *yet*," Perry responded. He put such malicious emphasis on the last word Emily clasped her arms closer around her chest. "If you'd prefer to be in that situation, I can oblige. I've got reasonable enough grounds to charge you with trespass and interfering with a police investigation."

"I didn't interfere with anything." Emily sat back in her chair and shot him a dirty look. "And how is it trespass when nobody told me I couldn't visit?"

"You were sneaking around at midnight. Do you seriously want to pretend you thought anyone at Stoneybrook Acres welcomed your night time escapade?"

"It's not even midnight now. You're exaggerating."

The PC flapped his hand at her—*whatever*. "If you don't want to talk to me now, then you can spend the night in a cell."

The choice didn't sound all that bad. As Emily's mouth split open into another gigantic yawn, she half closed her eyes and imagined the bliss of lying down. Then she sat straight up. No. It wouldn't do at all to walk out of the station tomorrow, with everyone knowing she'd spent the night.

Gossip was something to avoid at any cost.

"If I talk to you—even though it's the truth—you're not going to believe me." Emily also felt sure he'd make fun of her and the last thing her nerves needed was his raucous laughter.

"Try me." PC Perry sat back in his chair, arms folded. Hardly the picture of someone open to whatever Emily had to say.

"The sergeant will be better. We've already discussed some of what I'll say."

But Perry wasn't about to be put off. The glee on his face when he'd folded Emily into the back seat of the patrol car had told her everything she needed to know on that score.

She opened her mouth, almost ready to say the words, then closed her lips together in a hard line and shook her head. No. There was no chance he'd believe her, and she needed someone to take her seriously.

If her suspicions were correct, and the teenage ghosts she'd seen earlier this evening were buried on the property near the first body, then she needed a policeman who'd take action—not laugh.

"It's Sergeant Winchester or nobody. Arrest me if you're going to. Otherwise, let me go home and get some sleep."

Emily didn't expect the bluff to work. She'd already resigned herself to a night in a cell followed by an attempt to sneak out without anyone seeing her tomorrow.

"Fine. I'll let you go home for the night, but let me tell you"—PC Perry stabbed his finger towards her—"if I or any other officer catch you on the retirement home grounds again at night, you won't get the same leniency. You need to stay away from there and I don't expect to tell you again."

She could have argued the point but by now her brain was buzzing with lack of sleep. Emily nodded, trying her best to look chagrined, then followed him out of the interview room to the front desk.

"Sign here," the officer barked, pointing next to the entry logging her in. "No leaving town in the meantime. If you don't answer the sergeant when he calls in the morning, we'll put out an immediate alert."

Emily smiled at the thought she'd have anywhere else to go. The only people she knew—apart from a brother whose existence often slipped her mind altogether—lived and worked in Pinetar. If she turned up on the doorstep of her old colleagues from Christchurch, they'd be horrified.

A niggling part of her mind thought that would be a good enough reason to do just that. The more sensible half shut it down. A lack of sleep often engaged her sense of mischief but no good could come from roaming down that track.

"Thank you," Emily said, surprised at how heartfelt the simple statement of gratitude was. "When I talk to Sergeant Winchester, I'll be sure to mention how accommodating you were."

"Don't go overboard," Perry said, his nose wrinkling. Still, a small blush lit up his cheeks before she pushed away from the counter and opened the door.

As she stepped out into the cooling night air, Emily remembered her car was still parked on the road outside Stoneybrook. Luckily, her home wasn't too far away. A benefit of living in such a small town.

Sergeant Winchester got out of the car and walked around to the rear door to let Emily out. "I hope this doesn't backfire on me," he grumbled, as she clambered out with no grace.

Although she'd managed a few hours of sleep after PC Perry let her leave the station, morning had come far too quickly for Emily's body to recover fully. "I promise you, I'm not keen on anything that makes me appear foolish. Although I can't swear for certain there'll be anything there, nothing else makes sense."

"Believe me," the sergeant said, leading the way around the side of the home and along to the crime scene. "This doesn't make sense either. The sooner we get these spots dug up, the happier I'll be."

Emily had her mouth half opened to remind him that the police needed to investigate any reputable lead about a body. She closed it again because he was already doing that.

The fact Winchester chose to do it with such bad grace didn't matter.

"Right. Where are we digging?"

When she'd returned home the previous night, she'd expected her bedroom to be crowded out with all the spirits. Instead, not even Cynthia had made it back.

Apart from Peanut, who'd happily curled up on the bed next to her, she hadn't seen another ghost since.

Long may it last!

After taking a step back, Emily half closed her eyes to better remember the position of the boys the night before. She moved to the spot she recalled the first hand appearing and spun her heel in the lawn to make a mark. From there, she checked her position against the far wall and walked a few steps away to the second, then the third.

"And you're sure about this?" The sergeant glanced at her with a pleading expression. "If we start digging now, we'll have to include it on a report. It'll be added to the official case file for the original skeleton."

He didn't say the last words, but Emily heard it in her mind. *It'll never go away.*

"I'm sure."

While the sergeant signalled for the digging crew to begin, Emily walked to the entrance of Stoneybrook. She'd already checked with Winchester to make sure she didn't need to stay and watch throughout the entire thing. Given the strain of the previous day and night, she'd much rather wait inside and catch up with Agnes and Maude.

Margaret gave her a smile of recognition as Emily walked past her. She nodded back but didn't slow her gait. Luckily, Agnes had the door to her room ajar, so she didn't have to gather the courage to knock. The woman appeared pleased to see her and ushered her inside.

"So far, it's good news," Agnes said with a jerk of her chin towards Maude. "The director was in such a tizzy yesterday after the awful find and the police swarming about, he just told me to keep her out of the way until a final decision could be made.

"That's terrific. If he lets it go for a few days, it'll make it much harder to say no."

"And the woman from yesterday, Suzanne, she's changed her tune. Stopped by this morning to say how nice it'll be for Conker to have company."

"I bet she's hoping everyone puts out of their minds exactly what her dog had in his mouth!"

They giggled together, the horror of the situation igniting their sense of humour. Maude joined in, panting.

"What are they doing out there, today?" Agnes asked. "I saw you talking to the guy in charge earlier."

"Sergeant Winchester. They're digging in a few different spots, just to see if there's evidence they've missed."

"I hope today they also remember the pipe that caused the upheaval in the first place." Agnes patted her hair. "I couldn't stand to stay in the shower this morning. The water just dribbled out. I think if I'd washed my hair, I'd still be in there rinsing."

"Hm." Emily took a seat on the edge of the bed. "I bet the police either forgot or nobody informed them what the guy was doing here yesterday. They might've thought he was just breaking up the patio."

Agnes stood up, smoothing her skirts down and adjusting the neck of her blouse. "In that case, I'm going to talk to Mr Homeaway. I put up with this sort of nonsense when I was younger and couldn't afford any better. There's no reason for me to suffer quietly when I'm paying out an arm and a leg."

Maude jumped up with an alert expression on her face as Agnes walked out of the room. After a moment, Emily shrugged and also tagged along.

Allain wasn't in his office and Margaret didn't know where he'd gone. "I saw him earlier, around the back in the hospital facility. He might still be hiding away down there."

It didn't help Emily any but luckily, Agnes knew the rooms the receptionist was talking about. "It's out the other side of the nurse's station," she explained as they headed along a different corridor. "They keep the assisted and unassisted rooms on opposite sides of the complex. I'm not sure why."

As they emerged into the second part of the Stoneybrook home, Emily understood completely why they kept the two halves separate. On this side, it looked like a zombie apocalypse had taken hold of the residents. She knew her limp got bad sometimes, but the shuffling walk common to the first half-dozen people was ridiculous.

As they walked farther into the halls, Emily edged closer to Agnes.

"I think there's a common room on this side, too," the older lady said as they took turns, seemingly at random. "Unless he's visiting a specific person, I'd guess we'll find Mr Homeaway in there."

Emily wished she'd stayed behind. The view out the window at the digging might be nerve-inducing but not nearly so much as walking about Stoneybrook on this side.

"Shall we go back?" she'd just asked when Agnes gripped her arm and pointed.

"Here we go. When I took the tour a month ago, I

thought I'd never get the handle of this layout but now I'm here, it's pretty straightforward."

Since Emily doubted she'd be able to find her way back, she kept mute and nodded.

The common room held a half-dozen people with room for another thirty or more. Each resident sat by themselves, some nodding along to music only they could hear, others staring intently at the new arrivals.

"What's wrong with them?" Emily asked a second before she flagged the question as rude.

Agnes gave her a sharp look but answered. "Most of the residents over this side suffer from dementia. There are varying levels but a lot of them require around the clock care."

Emily nodded, feeling the fear encasing her in a block of cold cement. *This will be you one day. Take a good look.*

A nurse walked up to them with a frown. "Can I help you with something?"

"I'm searching for Mr Homeaway. Margaret said she'd seen him come over here."

The nurse retreated half a step, her mouth twisting. "Not that I've seen. Have you tried outside? There's a bunch of activity going on in the garden." Her gaze travelled to a window along that side of the home where a woman was standing, staring at the lawn. "I'll be glad when they fix the pipes out there and move on. It's disturbing some of our residents."

"They've found—"

Emily cut off when Agnes gave her an elbow in the side. "Thanks anyway. Is it all right if we hang around for a while?"

The nurse shrugged. "As long as you don't bother anyone, it's free access."

She walked away, her sensible white shoes squeaking even though the floor was carpeted. Emily stared after her with a feeling of dread. *One day, she'll be the only person taking care of you.*

"I wonder if they've found anything," Agnes said as she crossed to the window. The woman there stepped aside but didn't tear her gaze away from the scene. "It's all such dreadful timing. I thought the worst I'd have to deal with this week was moving, not a view out onto an unmarked grave."

"The oak tree," the woman at the window said in a halting voice as Emily joined them.

She followed where the lady's trembling finger pointed. The large oak with the scars twisting around its lower trunk. "It's lovely, isn't it? I love when trees grow so large, they dwarf everything around them."

"Cut it down." The woman jabbed her finger in quick motions, her nail tapping off the window. "Chop the tree down."

Agnes laughed. "Well, that's you told, Emily. Not everyone shares your point of view."

The woman grew more animated. In a second, she was slapping her entire palm against the window. "Fetch the axe. Cut it down."

Emily took a step back, cupping her elbows. "Okay, I take it back. It's a horrible tree and someone should get rid of it."

Her words placated the elder woman and her arms dropped down to her side. "There's Fred."

Agnes arched her eyebrow as she studied the lady's face. "Who's Fred?" She looked back outside. "All I can see is policemen. Did you mean Bobbies?"

As Emily peered over the woman's shoulder, she saw

the male ghost from the night before standing in the middle of the activity. He clapped as one man loosened the soil with a long iron pole before another shovelled out the dirt.

She put a hand on the lady's shoulder and pointed at the ghost. "Is that Fred?"

The woman turned, her watery blue eyes taking a second to focus on Emily's face. She was halfway to a smile when her eyes widened, and she jerked away, banging once more on the window. "Fetch the axe."

The nurse from earlier poked her head out of the doorway to the medical station. "What's going on out here? Gladys, are these ladies bothering you?"

Gladys nodded vigorously while Emily took a step away, holding her hands up to either side. "We didn't mean to upset her."

"I don't think it was us," Agnes said with a hint of indignation. "That lot out there are the ones digging up the garden. If anyone's causing bother, it's them."

A yell from outside backed up her words. The man responsible ran over the far side of the property, leaping over a short gate beside a shed and pelting toward the group at a sprint.

Even through the glass, Emily could hear the words. "What d'you think you're doing?"

Sergeant Winchester stepped forward, a hand up signalling the man to stop. Instead, the runner sidestepped the officer and kept sprinting towards the excavation.

"You can't just go digging up my lawn. It took me ages to get it nice and tidy."

The new arrival stopped short when he reached the police tape and his mouth dropped open as he took in the broken chunks of concrete where there'd been a patio the day before.

"What have you done? That's the barbeque area. You can't just wander on here and start messing stuff about. I've worked weeks getting this area nice. Who gave you the authority to come in here and destroy all my hard work?"

"The owner of the property," the sergeant called out, striding towards the man and placing a firm hand on his shoulder. "Now, how about you follow me—?"

"I'm not going anywhere. I want you to stop all this at once. Why're you doing this?"

He was so distraught, Emily thought for one moment he was about to burst into tears.

"Who's that?" she asked Agnes.

"It's Eli Jamieson, the gardener," the nurse replied after a quick glance. "And it's time you two headed back to your own ward. I have enough trouble keeping tabs on the residents over this side without you upsetting them."

"We didn't—"

The nurse gave Emily such a harsh glare the words died in her throat. "I'm sorry," she said instead in a meek voice. "We'll head back."

"And don't bring your dog over here again," the nurse said with a sniff. "It's dirty. Now I'll have to get the janitor to clean down all the floors."

Agnes opened her mouth, an expression of fury transforming her features, but Emily pulled her away from the oncoming confrontation. "Don't worry. Maude doesn't like it over here any more than we do," she muttered, earning a quick snort from her friend.

"That woman. Honestly." Agnes set off at such a clip down the corridor, Emily struggled to keep pace. "I hope I die before I get sent into her care. What a witch!"

"I'm sure she cares a lot about her patients," Emily said, not at all certain but wanting to calm her friend. "Besides, we're still on the hunt for Mr Homeaway so staying there won't help at all."

"Hm." Agnes pursed her lips. "Yes, well I can't be running all over the place trying to track him down. I'm going to stick to my room and watch all the action unfolding in front of me."

"Can I come too?"

"Of course, you can. And Maude." The dog raised her face up with interest upon hearing her name. "You're allowed to come to. It'll be like a party." She wrinkled her nose. "Except without food or music or booze."

Emily was still laughing as they walked into Agnes room. Outside, the sergeant gesticulated wildly, his arms flapping out to each side like he was trying to fly.

"What now?" Agnes asked, sitting on the bed. "He looks upset."

"He does." Emily scanned the scene, registering the policemen had stopped digging while the gardener stood off to one side, scowling. "I wonder if they've found something."

Sergeant Winchester turned and spotted Emily in the window. He gestured for her to come outside and after excusing herself to Agnes, she joined him on the lawn.

"Well," he said in greeting, "you were right."

Although she'd guessed what had happened, Emily's stomach still formed a tight fist, aching. "Another skeleton?"

"Three more." The sergeant rubbed his hand over the back of his neck and sighed. "All of them teenagers."

CHAPTER SEVEN

*E*mily took the cup of tea out of Crystal Dreaming's hand. "It was awful," she declared, shivering before taking a big sip.

The medium had been the first person she thought of when the police excused her from Stoneybrook, and not just because she was Emily's business partner. The woman overflowed with empathy and she craved some of that right now.

"I can imagine," Crystal said, sitting opposite. "Sometimes I get overwhelmed in the graveyard where the dead actually belong. Coming across bodies out in the wild..." She gave a shudder.

"And they're children, which makes everything worse."

"Oh, don't." Crystal held up a hand. "You know, often I want the spirits to talk to me but this time I'll gladly abstain. I'm crying and I wasn't even there." She dabbed at the edge of her eyes with a dainty handkerchief.

"I hope this is what the ghost needed to move on," Emily said with a sigh, pulling at the curl by her ear. "Cynthia might have been maddening but this man, with his silence, has been far worse."

"It's strange that he's afflicted, even after he's passed on." Crystal stroked the edge of the heavy crystal ball on the table between them. "I don't believe I've heard of that in my circles before."

"Afflicted?"

"From what you've told me, it sounds as though he has memory troubles. It would explain why he could locate the young ghosts while being unable to tell you so much as his name."

Emily gave a slow nod, letting her mind mull it over. "Half of Stoneybrook caters to dementia patients needing full-time care. I expect he came from there."

"I suppose they'll have to relocate them all. It's a pity."

"What? Why?"

Crystal tilted her head to one side and frowned. "Because one of their residents was buried under the patio. They can hardly keep the place open if that happens. I expect the police will lay charges against the director."

"He didn't seem like the type to kill anyone." *Far too fussy. Allain would probably faint at the sight of blood.*

"Whether he did the deed or not, the buck still stops with him. I'm surprised the police haven't taken him into custody already. The new remains might date back well before his time, but your nameless ghost must be more recent."

Emily took another sip of her tea. "I thought they'd leave an arrest until they know for sure who put him there."

"But if he wasn't reported missing in the first place, then it's negligence." Crystal sat forward, hands pressed flat on the table. "And I know for a fact, there's been no one reported missing in Pinetar since a teenage girl back in the nineties."

Crystal shook her head, pulling her lips into a prim line.

"We all pitched in back then to join the foot search and we would've done the same for a missing dementia patient. I can't believe the heartlessness of the man to let someone wander off and never bother to report it."

"We don't know that's what happened. You're just guessing."

"I'd like to know another explanation for how he wound up there."

But Emily couldn't answer that one and fell silent. She'd already tried to think of an innocent explanation and couldn't get very far. If only her ghost had been more vocal, she'd be able to pick a side and join in with the calls for arrest or offer up a decent rebuttal.

"The ghost appears to be in his seventies or older," Emily said. "Whatever happened didn't cut much off his life." She held up a hand before Crystal could get started. "I understand that's no excuse, but the teenagers worry me a lot more than he does."

"Please, don't." Crystal's face drained of colour and she pulled at the lobe of her right ear. "I mean it when I say I can't bear to think about them."

"Okay. How's the felting club going?"

Crystal immediately brightened. "Now that Diane has taken the reigns of leadership, we're doing much better. I hardly notice Hilda's absence these days."

They chatted for a while, finishing off their cups of tea and musing on lighter subjects. By the time Emily excused herself to go to work, she felt on a much more even keel.

At the charity shop, Pete appeared happy to see her. He filled her in with the morning's clients of note—a boy who came in each week to trade the second-hand book he'd just read for a new one, an old lady searching for porcelain thimbles—and Emily relaxed.

After a short struggle up the stairs out the back to the attic, she shut the door and got to work sorting out the latest donation boxes while Gregory was out and about, collecting still more. While sorting out a few treasures from the majority of trash, she even managed a smile.

Peanut was so affectionate from the moment Emily stepped foot inside the door, she immediately knew something was wrong.

"Hello?" she called out, hesitating by the entrance, half wanting to head out and leave whatever waited for her until later. A sigh came from down the hall and she raised her eyebrows at Peanut, then pulled the door closed and followed the noise.

"Nice to see you again." Emily gave a small wave to the male ghost when she found him seated on the windowsill in her bedroom.

He gave a start and stood up, bowing and wringing his hands together.

"I guess you weren't here about the boys, then." Emily gave her own sigh and kicked her shoes off. "Any chance you can tell me your name?"

The man clenched his hands so tightly, Emily winced. If she tried that her arthritis would scream for a week. He opened his mouth, leaning forward, and she mimicked the posture, ears attuned for the slightest whisper. With a frustrated twist of his lips, the ghost sat back, loosening his hands long enough to thump on his leg.

"Don't worry about it," Emily said, ignoring the twist of concern gripping her chest. "It'll come when it's ready. I'm about to make my dinner, so if you want company, I'll be in the kitchen."

When she walked in the room, Peanut scampered out from behind the rubbish bin. "What's up with you, little fella? Don't you like our new guest?"

Apparently not, since the ghost cat ran to a new hiding place behind the sofa as the man shuffled into the kitchen.

"Keep to one side," Emily warned. "I don't want to drop anything because of you giving me a fright."

Unable to keep silent with a guest standing so near, she embarked on a tale of everything that had happened since she'd left Stoneybrook Acres. Since the ghost had been in the gardens of the home, she supposed he knew all about that part of the day.

When her chicken and steamed vegetables were ready, Emily moved to the sofa to eat while watching the news. The ghost trudged behind her and after she'd been sitting for a minute, perched on the edge of a chair.

The headlines showed the world was in much the same position as the news the night before had left it. No notice about buried skeletons in Pinetar but she supposed the police might want to keep that under wraps.

It would be hard enough to investigate four cold cases without a barrage of media trailing them at every step.

She kept the television on, muted until the weather. After the meteorologist ran through the main centres, Emily kept her eyes fixed to the scrolling bar along the bottom. One of her favourite games was 'how hot is my town compared to everyone else's.' In the winter, the goal would flip, but the game would otherwise remain the same.

As the ticker tape reached the city of Wellington, the ghost became animated. He pointed to the television, then his chest, repeating the gesture until it resembled a large tremor.

"What is it?" Emily put the last of her meal aside and leaned toward him, scanning the ghost's face for some hint of what he was thinking. "Is that where you're from?"

He nodded and shook his head, his gestures slowing as the weather report headed further south. A forlorn expression suffused his face, so painful that Emily had to glance away.

"How about I do the dishes, then we'll talk?"

She didn't look to the ghost for an answer, keeping her head down as she went into the kitchen. Peanut was once again hiding in there, this time with his back half inside the ajar pantry door while his front paws were just outside.

"Do you think you're food, now?" Emily cast an amused glance his way while she waited for the water to run hot. "If you stay there, somebody might mistake you for a sack of potatoes."

Peanut flicked his ears towards her but otherwise remained unresponsive. When Emily shook her hand through the sink water to raise some bubbles, she cupped a handful and blew them his way.

"Still nothing, huh? I've got to tell you, between your mood and the other one, I've got a tough crowd tonight."

She finished up and pulled out an antique she'd brought home with her from the charity shop. When Emily had opened a box in the late afternoon, she'd at first thought someone had thrown in a twisted typewriter keyboard with the case missing. On closer inspection, she was delighted to uncover a Blickensderfer typewriter No 5.

The keyboard needed a good polish and the type wheel ball looked on its last legs, but Pete had verified the model used the scientific layout for keys. Emily hoped with a careful clean, it might fetch up to a thousand dollars at auction.

Or it might not. Even after a few months in the role, it took Emily by surprise how variable bidders were, especially when an antique took their fancy.

As she laid out a soft cleaning cloth and Brasso cream, the ghost ambled over to stare at the contraption. He pointed at the keys, giving a soft hoot—the first sound she'd heard him make since the night before.

"Do you like that? Were you a typist or a journalist or something?" She scanned his face for a reaction but saw no change.

When she tried to move him aside to sit down, the ghost continued to stand and point at the typewriter. When she worked out he was pointing at different keys, in turn, Emily felt like slapping her forehead. Doh!

Unsure if the machine would work, she scrolled in a piece of paper and stood back, letting the ghost point to the different keys. As she hit them, unknown squiggles appeared on the paper. When even Emily could see the words repeating, she pulled the paper out.

With over a year of experience to teach her how debilitating illiteracy was, Emily's phone now sported every app possible to aid her in having a normal life. She scrolled through the tiny icons now, giving a triumphant call when she found the right one.

Using the camera, she lined up the paper on the screen and let the computer read the words back to her. Frederick Wilmott. Over and over.

"That's your name?" Emily checked with the ghost. "Frederick Wilmott?"

He nodded, an expression of profound relief crossing his face.

She bent her head to the side, studying him, unable to tell if he knew a lot more than he was letting on. A ghost who could pick their name out on a typewriter, but not just say it. If it was a trick of his mind, the universe must be having a laugh, teaming him up with an illiterate.

But he clapped his hands together softly, beaming a smile. Wasn't that irony just the way the universe liked to work?

Emily sighed and flicked through her phone until it showed a picture of Sergeant Winchester. Hopefully, with a name, they could sort the case out and return the ghost to his rightful home.

CHAPTER EIGHT

When Sergeant Winchester pulled up outside Stoneybrook Acres, he turned off the engine but continued to sit in the car.

"Is there something wrong?" Emily asked from the back seat. She was trapped unless he came around to open her door. The thought he might zone out and leave her seated there for hours zipped through her mind.

He turned around, bracing his hand on the passenger headrest. "It might be best if you don't speak unless I specifically ask you something."

The sting of his words hit Emily full-force. Her day hadn't been conducive to taking shots on the jaw. Not that she showed that to him. Instead, she lifted her chin and plastered on her widest smile. "Don't worry. The crazy ghost lady won't speak unless spoken to."

The sergeant appeared as though he was about to add something, then shook his head and got out of the car. He let Emily out of the back seat, and she stretched her legs while he checked the perimeter of the police taped area—greatly expanded during the day.

"Okay, let's see what information we can get out of the night staff."

Emily gave a start as she realised how late it was. Of course, she'd finished eating her tea before the adventures in point-typing began but, for some reason, her mind was stuck in the late afternoon.

Margaret Tillerson had packed up her reception desk and gone for the day. In her stead was a man dressed in a blue uniform. His mouth hung ajar, and he pulled at his earlobe as the sergeant advanced on him with a stern expression.

"We need your help to source information on a previous resident." Sergeant Winchester tapped his police ID on the counter, flipping it closed and tucking it in his trouser pocket before the man even thought to glance down.

"Sure. Whatever I can do to help." The man ran a hand through his hair and pulled the computer keyboard close. He tapped in a few digits, then frowned at the screen. "Just a moment."

As he opened a drawer and rifled through the contents, Emily saw an elderly woman coming down the corridor. A smile crossed her face as she thought it was Agnes, then the woman glanced up. No. A stranger. The lady turned off into a room and slammed the door.

"Margaret must've changed the password," the man said, half under his breath. "If you don't mind waiting, I'll give her a call."

"Sure, take your time," the sergeant said, his voice laden with irony. He stood back, staring at his watch with a frown. "What's your name, son?"

"Erik Asgood," the man replied. He tucked the receiver of the phone between his ear and shoulder, extending a hand for the sergeant to shake. "Sorry about this, but we don't often have late callers. Manning the desk after hours is usually just helping the residents back to bed when they go wandering."

His attention was diverted as someone answered his call, and he hurriedly explained the problem, scribbling on the desk pad as he did so. A few seconds later, Erik's fingers flew over the keyboard again and he hung up the phone. "We're in."

"What information do you have in there?" the sergeant asked, leaning over the counter so the screen was in view. "How old was this fellow?"

"Seventy-two at his last birthday," Erik replied.

As Emily wandered back to the desk, he hunched his shoulders, shielding the screen. She smiled to herself. *Needn't bother on my account.*

"He's from around Pinetar, I take it?"

To the sergeant's surprise, the answer to that was no. "The address on file from before he moved in here is in Tawa, in Wellington." Erik shrugged. "That is a bit odd, but I suppose we have residents in here from all over. Sometimes, folks like to move somewhere quieter in their twilight years."

"Does it mention his occupation?"

The man shook his head, frowning as he clicked and typed. "I'll print out what we have, but it's not big on those sorts of details. The home is more interested in whether they can afford to pay for ongoing care and meet the monthly fees than anything else."

There was a sudden noise behind Emily, and she jumped, whirling on her heels. The printer spat out sheets of paper in fits and starts and she gave a small laugh, feeling silly.

Erik tapped on the keyboard again. "Oh, now this bit is

interesting—"

"Erik," Margaret called out as she strode through the doorway. "How about you move over and let me search out the information?" She nodded to the sergeant and offered a conspiratorial smile. "I'm far more used to pulling up our resident's details than he is."

Although the man stood and moved back, Emily could read from the expression on his face that he wasn't pleased with the interruption. "I was doing fine—"

"I'm sure you were. Now, who did you want information on?"

Emily paused for a second, ensuring nobody was looking in her direction, then she moved to the corner and lifted all the sheets from the printer. If anybody had asked, she would have turned them straight over, but the sergeant was now barking a series of questions at Margaret.

"I can't tell you that!" the receptionist said with a gasp of horror, pressing a hand up to her throat. "It's more than my job's worth to pass on that kind of personal information. I'm the one who set up everything to keep in good standing with the privacy principals. Unless you have a warrant?"

Margaret raised her eyebrows at the sergeant, who gruffly admitted he didn't. Behind her, Erik flushed a deep crimson. He backed up a few steps, then turned and scurried down the corridor. Emily took the opportunity to shove all the papers into her handbag. She could hand them to the sergeant later, outside.

"We're not going to misuse the information," the sergeant explained in a slow voice.

Over the past year, Emily had been on the receiving end of that tone more than she liked to admit. If it got her back up, it certainly wouldn't endear Margaret to him.

As if reading her mind, the woman sniffed and folded

her arms. "I'm not silly, Sergeant Winchester. I know what's allowed to be divulged without our patient's permission and what's not. Don't think you can bully me into breaking the law."

"But you'll have to hand it over when I get the warrant tomorrow," the sergeant mansplained to her while Emily winced. "All you're doing is postponing the inevitable."

"All I'm doing is protecting our resident's privacy until you fetch the correct paperwork saying I don't have to." Margaret had a biro in her hand and now she pointed it directly between the sergeant's eyes. "Just because it's expedient for you not to follow protocol, doesn't mean I have to oblige."

Sergeant Winchester held up his hands and back a step away from the counter. "Fine. What are you allowed to tell me about Frederick Wilmott, then?"

A micro-expression of satisfaction skipped across Margaret's face, then was gone. In its place was an overdone frown. "Why do you want to know?"

The sergeant swallowed, his Adam's apple bobbing up and down. He placed his hands flat on the counter and leaned forward. "Because there's a dead body buried under Stoneybrook's patio and I'd like to identify the deceased."

Margaret's eyes narrowed. "And you think Fred had something to do with that?" She clicked her tongue. "I doubt it. The man must be in his seventies by now. Hardly strong enough to kill someone, let alone bury them under a load of concrete."

"We don't think he killed anybody." Winchester shot a confused glance in Emily's direction.

She felt a twinge of discomfort as the same emotion bloomed in her mind.

Now, Margaret faltered. "Then why do you want to

know about him?" Her gaze flicked to Emily before returning to the sergeant.

Winchester's lips tightened with a grimace of satisfaction. "I'm afraid I can't divulge that information. Official police business, you know."

Emily stepped forward, a terrible thought clouding her mind. "Can you tell us if Frederick Wilmott was a resident here?"

"What do you mean 'was?' As far as I know, he still is." Margaret shook her head and glanced across the blotter page in front of her. "At least, he was this morning."

Sergeant Winchester closed his eyes for a moment, drawing an audible breath in through his nose. "Frederick Wilmott is a current resident of Stoneybrook Acres, is that what you're saying?"

"Yes, of course." Margaret's frown grew so deep her forehead appeared folded. "He's suffering from dementia so I'm not sure how much he could answer, but you're free to question him directly if you want. Room twenty-four."

CHAPTER NINE

Sergeant Winchester dropped Emily at home without another word spoken between them. Part of her wanted to apologise for the wasted time but another felt aggrieved.

It wasn't as though she held herself out to be the world's leading expert on ghost interpretation. What she knew, she'd passed on. If the dead man wanted to spell words out on a typewriter that only led to further riddles, that was his prerogative.

If the sergeant had any clues at all, he wouldn't have jumped on her sole piece of information. There must have been plenty of dud leads he'd proposed during his time on the force—she wouldn't say sorry just because one of hers led nowhere.

All the justification left Emily in a fine grump by the time she let herself into the house. Peanut jumped onto her legs the moment she walked through the door, and it took a lot of restraint not to burst into tears.

"Hey, there. You want to sit on my lap while I watch some mindless telly?"

From the expression of adoration on Peanut's face, Emily presumed he did.

"Thank goodness you're home," Cynthia called out as she walked into the lounge.

Taking a second to remove her heart from her mouth, Emily returned the greeting. The male ghost was also in attendance, sitting right in the place she'd intended to lie down.

Unwilling to disturb his silent presence, Emily sat on a dining room chair instead. Peanut jumped into her lap and curled up, his purr sending a pleasant reverberation through her legs.

"The old mime-act and I have been having a marvellous conversation." Cynthia rolled her eyes. "So far, I've told him all about my childhood and the proper maintenance routine for a lady to keep her skin glowing past the age of twenty-five. In return, he's told me—oh, what was it again?" She placed a forefinger along the side of her cheek, staring up the ceiling, then snapped her fingers. "That's it. Nothing. Nothing at all."

Emily leaned to her side and snagged the typewriter. "He spelled out a name earlier using this," she said, waving a hand over the contraption. "If you're going to hang out here, perhaps it's worth another try?"

"What name?" Cynthia asked, then held a hand over her mouth. "Or don't you know."

"I know. I'm illiterate, not incapable. According to my app, he pointed out the name Frederick Wilmott." She pulled down the corner of her mouth. "Unfortunately, it turns out that's not *his* name."

"Curiouser and curiouser. Who was it then?" Cynthia's eyes grew wide. "Was it his murderer?"

"Not by the sounds of it. I thought it was him"—Emily

jerked her head at the ghost—"until the receptionist at Stoneybrook told me they have a resident called that who's alive and well. She also said, since he's past seventy and part of their dementia wing, it's unlikely he could murder someone and bury their body."

"You never know. Just because someone's old, you shouldn't write them off completely." A shadow passed over Cynthia's features. "I learned that to my detriment."

"Not everyone old is a murderer." Emily stroked Peanut, feeling the gentlest whisper of his presence under her hand—the most solidity the ghost cat could manage.

"How about it, old chap?" she said, turning to the elderly man. "Do you feel up to spelling out something more? A clue, perhaps?"

Long minutes passed as the ghost continued to stare straight ahead. Emily was about to suggest she'd head off to bed when he moved. After a shambling walk to the typewriter, he gestured at the keys again.

"A," Cynthia called out, finally becoming useful. "S. T. R. I. D."

The second time through, Emily clicked her fingers. "Astrid. I used to go to school with a girl named that."

"How about a surname, old chum?" Cynthia gave a ghost a friendly elbow in the side. "There's no use in keeping secrets now. Not when you're stone-cold dead."

But even that cheerful sentiment couldn't sway him from repeating the same name again. Cynthia pouted and grew bored. "I don't like your new friend," she said with a sniff, turning back to Emily. "I think he's broken. You should send him back and get a replacement."

"I should send *you* back," Emily said, covering a gigantic yawn with her hand. "You're meant to be at peace in whatever passes for an afterlife."

After that, Cynthia bit her tongue for a while.

There was a list of things Emily should do, chief amongst them, cleaning up the typewriter for sale. Instead, she sat in the chair, stroking Peanut and letting her mind wander. With all the stress and excitement of the past few days, it was nice to relax and think about nothing.

Close to sleep, Emily remembered the papers in her purse. With the detente between her and the sergeant on the ride back, she'd forgotten to pass them along.

"How do you feel about some light reading?" she asked Cynthia. "We might find something useful in here to send our new guest on his way."

She spread the printout on the table and let Cynthia peruse them. Emily had left enough room for the typewriter at the side, but still, the woman nudged the man along until he returned to his earlier spot on the sofa.

"It's not very enthralling," Cynthia said after a few minutes of speed-reading. "Frederick Wilmott moved into Stoneybrook Acres four years ago and promptly deteriorated. I'd say the reason was financial stress, these monthly fees are so high, except it looks like he qualified for government assistance."

Emily gave a chuckle. "The night staff guy who printed these out said the retirement home was only concerned with whether its residents could afford to pay them each month."

"They have gone into a lot of detail on that front," Cynthia agreed. "Oh, this one's a bit different. It says he qualifies for a benefit because he used to be a pupil at the Oakhaven School."

"Really?" Emily sat up straight, much to Peanut's displeasure. "That's the school that ran in the grounds before Stoneybrook reinvented itself as a retirement community."

"That grim place was a school?" Cynthia shuddered.

"Does it say what years?"

"No. It just mentions the benefit." She shuffled through the remaining pages. "You could try to find out more on the internet."

"I suppose I could." Emily dragged her laptop out and spoke a variety of voice commands into the search engine. "Here's something," she said after twenty minutes of useless results. "I think it's a school roll."

She pressed the command for the computer to begin reading it out, but it got stuck on the description.

After a frustrated minute, Cynthia sighed and walked over. "Just pull it up on screen and I'll read it through."

Emily opened it up and put the image on full-screen. "Thanks. These archives really need to be updated for use by everybody."

Cynthia gave a soft snort. "Yeah. I'm sure they'll get right on that. Considering they're only a tiny fraction of a percentage of getting things scanned and uploaded onto the internet, I'm sure voice support is coming any day now."

With a shrug of her shoulder, Emily abandoned the conversation. "If you can find Astrid or Frederick on there, it should give us a start."

"He's here," Cynthia said in surprise. She pointed to a line with the tip of a manicured fingernail. "This is Frederick Wilmott and here's Astrid Wallheimer."

Emily sat up, gazing at the screen as though looking closer would somehow lend the squiggles sense. "What other names are listed?"

As Cynthia read through the names, Emily gave a start at one. "Gladys. There's a woman at Stoneybrook Acres with the same name. It's unusual enough it could be the same person."

"Maybe."

Cynthia finished off the remaining list, forty-four in total, but no others twigged a response. Emily instructed the computer to search for Gladys Angel. Amongst the images that showed up, she recognised the woman from the home.

"It's strange that two pupils ended up back in the same place they'd spent their school years in," she mused.

"Not really." Cynthia moved back to the paperwork on the table, nudging the male ghost aside. "If they're receiving a benefit devised specifically for ex-students—or inmates—of Oakhaven School, then it stands to reason they'd return there. According to this, it only supports them at the same establishment."

"Do you think a local philanthropist made it available?"

The computer soon assured them money was issued from a trust set up by the ex-headmaster of Oakhaven, Samuel Leuf.

As Emily's yawns grew more frequent, she called it a night. "Tomorrow, I'll visit Stoneybrook to talk to Frederick Wilmott and Gladys Angel. Hopefully, they'll know something more."

"If they're on the dementia ward, it won't matter." Cynthia waved her hand at the male ghost, who swayed to and fro beside the table. "Any information is probably locked up tight, without the capacity to retrieve it."

"Well, I'd like to find out either way."

As Emily pulled back the covers to get into bed, she found herself facing an audience of three. Peanut, she didn't mind, and patted the bedspread to encourage him to join her. The other two she wasn't nearly so comfortable with.

"Couldn't you take him to the lounge?" Emily asked.

"No offence, old fella but I don't relish the thought of you staring at me while I'm sleeping."

With a grumble, Cynthia tugged the man's hand until he obediently followed her into the other room.

Emily lay on her back for a moment before turning out the light, relishing the vibrations as Peanut's tiny motor purred. Instead of solving a mystery, she just seemed to have opened another can of worms.

Her stomach tightened at the thought of talking to Gladys and Frederick tomorrow. When she switched off the lamp and closed her eyes, she saw the shuffling motions of the dementia sufferers, so like the infected on The Walking Dead.

Well, she could put up with it in order to see what information they were holding. The image of Gladys from earlier in the day blinked into her mind—*cut it down*. Whatever the woman had been peering out at through the window had been overlaid with another image, the past playing out over the present as though they were compatible timelines.

With a sigh, Emily turned over in bed, adjusting the ghost cat and her pillow. A soft noise caught her attention just as most of her mind tried to pull her into sleep.

She opened her eyes, expecting to see a curtain swaying in the breeze from the ajar window. The male ghost stared straight at her, his face only inches away.

Emily huffed out a breath, her chest too tight to scream. The man's eyes never wavered, staying fixed on her face even though he must come from a generation taught not to stare.

"Please sit further away if you're going to stay in here," Emily said, her voice so weak the order turned into a plea. It was no wonder that the ghost didn't comply.

She turned to face the wall, even though her breath bouncing back of its surface made her feel claustrophobic. With the weight of the man's eyes resting on the back of Emily's head, even her exhaustion struggled to cart her away to sleep.

CHAPTER TEN

The following day was Thursday, so Emily spent the morning at the Pinetar auction house, preparing second-hand goods for sale. The sales room was more crowded than usual, so Emily had to wait for a while for an assistant to write out the labels for her items and tag the entire box.

Once done, she skipped her lunch in favour of calling in on Crystal and roping her into paying a visit to Stoneybrook Acres. After a poor night's sleep—with dreams of a monster staring blankly at her—Emily didn't want to venture into the dementia ward alone.

She already held some trepidation about the outing. There was no need to cancel it due to her jitters when she could instead call upon a friend to hold her hand.

They'd just arranged to meet at Crystal's after Emily finished work for the day when she was booted out of the house by clients turning up early for a reading. After a short chat with Pete, Emily mounted the stairs to the airless attic, wishing it were winter when the room would be snug instead of confining.

"Back again," Margaret said a few hours later as Emily approached the front desk. "If you spend any longer here, I'll have to issue you with a room."

"You're working late," Emily said, trying not to shudder at the thought. "I hope we didn't ruin your night too much, yesterday."

"Not at all," the receptionist replied, although the large sigh accompanying the statement told a different story. "Are you here to visit Agnes?"

Emily was about to say no, then thought twice and nodded. She didn't want to get into a discussion of who could and couldn't receive visitors. Although she didn't know the protocol for the retirement complex, it seemed unlikely Margaret would be thrilled if she asked to see the same man she'd been enquiring about the night before.

"What a surprise," Agnes said when they knocked on her door. "Maude, see who's come to visit."

Maude raised her eyebrows in their direction but didn't bother to raise her head.

"I don't think she's enjoying it here much," Agnes whispered. "She used to like to trot around the back yard for most of the day, coming in and out of the house as she fancied. Being trapped in here with me doesn't suit her at all."

"We can take her for a walk," Emily offered, spotting an opportunity. "It's no bother, and I'd hate to think of Maude moping when she's lucky to be here at all."

This time, she thought to ask for a leash for the bulldog. With it safely clipped to the collar, Emily, Crystal, and Maude set off into the gardens, giving the holes near the patio a wide berth.

The worker from a few days before was there. From the long excavation trench leading away from the police tape,

Emily surmised he'd finally been allowed to complete his work.

"Did you get the pipe sorted?" she asked as Maude dragged her toward the man.

"All done," he said with a nod, wiping his hands on a rag pulled from his pocket. "I've just got to fill all the dirt back in tomorrow, then I never need to visit here again."

"I'm sorry," Emily said, shaking her head. "It's an awful experience for you, too. I know the residents"—she nodded at the shadow of Agnes, staring out from her window—"will be very glad to have the water back up to full pressure. Apparently, showers have become quite a chore."

The man chuckled more than the comment deserved. "Well, they don't need to worry on that score any longer. Full pressure has been restored."

Emily gave a nod and moved on, finding Crystal staring with maudlin fascination at the series of holes. Despite the tape and plastic huts placed over the work, it was still easy to peer through the openings and see exactly what was going on. A PC standing guard near the site gave them both a careful side-eye.

"Can you imagine living here for years, then finding out there was a graveyard in the back garden nobody knew about?" The medium shook her head, hugging herself despite the warmth of the day.

"Hardly a graveyard," Emily said, letting Maude lead them away from the site. "Those bodies were being hidden, not interred."

"Do you think the mafia moved into Pinetar while we weren't looking?"

Emily screwed up her nose and uttered a small laugh. "No, I don't think so. For one, the local gangs wouldn't tolerate them moving onto their patch and for another, I can't imagine what an old man or teenagers would need to do to get themselves assassinated."

"Maybe they were drug mules."

"Maybe someone should put her imagination to rest."

Crystal bent to pick a bright pink flower from the spray of valerian growing wild along the edge of the woodland. She sniffed it as they walked the border of the property, waiting for Maude to grow tired.

"I should pick some of those for their roots," Emily said, cupping a hand over her mouth to catch a yawn. "If I don't get a good night's sleep soon, I'll be laid up by this time next week."

"Restless spirits keeping you awake, are they?" Crystal smiled but a hint of envy escaped in her voice.

Emily nodded. "When I wished for a man in my bedroom, this wasn't quite what I had in mind."

It took her a second, then Crystal burst into laughter. "Oh, my," she said, fanning herself. "Now, I've come over all peculiar."

"Could you take Maude's lead?" Emily asked, handing it over before Crystal had a chance to answer. "I'm getting a cramp."

She plonked herself down, crushing half a dozen different species of wildflower. The large muscle along her right thigh stiffened into a slab of rock, and for the next few minutes, Emily couldn't think past the pain.

When the limb finally eased up, she gave a shaky laugh. "I really wish these things would give me a written warning." She took Crystal's offer of a hand, and stood up, shifting her weight slowly from one foot to the other.

"We can go in the back of the home," Crystal said, pointing. "That'll be quicker than walking all the way around the outside."

"I hope you've got a better sense of direction than me," Emily said, nodding to the suggestion. "The corridors from this side to the other are like a spider's web."

"What? Sticky?"

Emily was still giggling when she reached the door to the hospital side of the retirement home. She grabbed the handle, then frowned and tugged again, harder.

"It's locked," she said in bewilderment. "Why would they do that?"

"It's getting late," Crystal said, checking her watch. "Well, it's after six-thirty."

Emily raised her eyebrows as she knocked on the door.

"It's late when you're old," Crystal said in a defensive tone. "If you eat your dinner at three thirty, the long summer evenings just drag on forever."

The nurse Emily had met the day before poked her head out. "What are you doing out here? This isn't a public entrance."

"I'm sorry, my leg cramped, and I wondered if we could use this as a short-cut."

The nurse frowned at Emily for so long, she half expected the door to slam in her face. Then the woman sighed and stood back to let them pass. "You want to take magnesium to stop that happening. Adding bananas or salmon to your diet will clear that right up."

After they were through the door, the nurse locked it again. Emily frowned but didn't pursue the issue, despite the large green exit sign hanging from the ceiling above them.

"Is Frederick Wilmott or Gladys Angel about?" she asked instead. "I'd love the chance to talk to them."

The nurse waved at two doors down opposite corridors. "They'll be in their rooms. We don't stay up late in this wing. Most of the residents wake up before sunrise so they go to bed early."

"Frederick's in room twenty-four, isn't he?" Emily recalled Margaret's words from last night.

The nurse nodded but frowned. "You can't take the dog in there. Our residents often experience anxiety and I'm sure an animal will upset them."

Emily's immediate opinion was the opposite, but she nodded, ready to give up the idea.

Crystal tugged Maude a few steps away. "I'll take her back to Agnes and have a chat about how she's settling in here. I haven't caught up with her since she stopped being able to come to felting club."

She headed off and gratitude surged through Emily's chest until it glowed. "I'll meet you there, later." It hadn't even occurred to her that Agnes and Crystal might already be friends.

Emily knocked on Frederick Wilmott's door, holding her breath while she waited for an answer. When he told her to come in, she opened the door slowly, giving him a chance to get himself decent if he wasn't already.

"Frederick Wilmott?"

"Who're you?"

The sharp tone caught Emily off-guard. She'd been expecting more of a befuddled air, similar to her ghost companion. For a second, her own name stuck on the end of her tongue, leaving her stuttering. "E... E... Emily."

Mr Wilmott's room was the exact same layout as Agnes's and he sat in the chair next to the desk, his head tilted to one side. "Nice to meet you, E-E-Emily," he said, the mocking softened by a large smile. "What brings you to my bachelor pad at this time of night?"

"I was hoping to ask you a few questions if you don't

mind." Her hands wrung together, the knuckles protesting. "About when you were at—Oh!"

She saw the framed photograph sitting in pride of place on the man's desk. An old school photograph with students lined up in neat rows, either grinning or scowling.

The quality of the image was terrible, half of the students faces eradicated by the smear of movement. The varnished wooden frame had worn away over years of use, revealing the original light-coloured flesh beneath the stain.

"Writing up a history of the school, are you?" Mr Wilmott asked, passing the photograph across to her. "If so, I can't help you out, I'm afraid." He rapped the side of his head with a knuckle. "This old case is mostly empty."

The wit behind his pronouncement and the twinkle in the man's eye belied the words. Emily took quick peeks at his face in between studying the photograph. If this man actually suffered from confusion or memory loss, she'd eat her hat.

"What about the people in this photo? Can you tell me who they are?"

He shook his head, holding a hand out for her to return the picture but she kept hold of it, turning it over to inspect the back. A long-held habit formed by years of treasure hunting through auctions or pawing through garage sales on the weekend.

A list, probably of names, was written in pencil, now so faded it blurred into smudges. Emily bit her lip in a burst of frustration. Even if the marks were legible, they wouldn't tell her anything. She handed it back to the man, pointing to the scribbles. "You don't need to rely on your memory."

A quick frown creased his brow then was lost in the reappearance of a sunny smile. "Fine, it's my old gang from when I attended this place the first time. Under duress."

"You're here willingly, now?"

Emily had meant the question as a joke, but the locked door intruded on her thoughts and soured her tone. He jerked back as though she'd struck out at him.

"Yes, I am. They take good care of me here. Nurse Rebecca is an absolute doll."

His tone was so defensive, she could tell Mr Wilmott meant every word. Still, Emily found it hard to reconcile the word doll with the stern woman she'd met twice.

"I'm sorry." Emily tried a smile on for size, running a hand through her hair and blowing out a breath. "I think we got off on the wrong foot. Can we start again?"

"No. I don't think we can." Mr Wilmott stood, towering a good six inches above her. Sat down, he hadn't looked anywhere near that tall. "I'd like you to leave. It's been a very tiring day and I need to get some rest."

"Just one thing," Emily held up a finger as he went to push her back towards the door. "Can you tell me Gladys Angel's room number?" When he hesitated, she lied, "I picked up something of hers by accident yesterday and need to return it."

"She's in room thirteen. It's down the corridor opposite." He gave a sad smile. "We're not trustworthy enough to have men and women on the same side."

Before he could advance on her again, Emily left and hurried to Gladys's room. The entire affair seemed an exercise in futility, but she forced herself to knock.

"Can you let me out?" a small voice whispered from the other side. It sounded like the woman must be pressed up tight against the door. "They don't let me have a key."

Emily turned the handle, her mouth falling open as it met resistance. To lock the exit door was bad enough, but to lock a resident in her room was unforgivable. She turned around, ready to stampede down the hallways to the nurse's station. Nurse Rebecca stood right behind her, holding a key.

"You'll need this," she said shortly, unlocking the door and pocketing the key again. "Don't keep her up too late and if she gets upset, call me."

The woman strode away, gone around the corner before Emily could quite work out what was happening. She opened the door with care. Gladys crowded her as soon as it opened.

"Are you here to take me home?" she whispered, bright spots lighting up on her cheeks like an old-fashioned doll. "I don't want to stay here."

"Can you help me out with a few questions?" Emily asked, ignoring the hope in the woman's eyes. "Do you remember when you were at school here?"

Confusion clouded Gladys's eyes. "School. I didn't go to school." She stamped her foot on the floor. "I've been held in this prison ever since I was a little girl and I want to go home!"

With the woman's voice rising, so too did Emily's sense of alarm. She held her hands up, shushing the woman as she took another step into the room.

"You're not with them, are you?"

"No." Emily shook her head in an overly large gesture, sending her hair flying into her eyes. "I'm not. Do you remember Frederick Wilmott?"

"Fred sent you?" Gladys went very still, her eyes as wide as saucers. "Did he make it to Astrid in time?"

"I'm sure he did." Emily thought about the school roll printout in her bag. She wouldn't be able to read the answers even if Gladys could make head or tail of them. Still... It was what she'd come here to do. Talking to this time-confused woman wouldn't get them anywhere but a name might.

"You remember Astrid and Fred, but can you tell me about the other students you attended Oakhaven with?"

Emily sat on the bed and patted the cover next to her. When Gladys perched beside her, she handed over the paper and a pen. "You remember the boys buried out in the back garden, don't you?"

Gladys jerked her head up to stare at Emily, her mouth pulled down in despair. "We're not allowed to talk about that," she said in a whisper, then checked over her shoulder. "You remember what Mr Leuf said?"

"What did he say?"

When tears welled in Gladys's eyes, Emily reached for her hand and squeezed it gently. "He can't hurt you. Not now. Tell me what he said."

She felt an utter bully, pressuring the woman even that little bit, but Emily's selfishness forced her onwards. She didn't want to spend another night in the same room as a man who stared at her intently while she slept. The thought sent a zap of electricity racing over her scalp, tingling unpleasantly.

"No one will believe us, anyway. It's no use telling anyone." Gladys pulled her hand free and picked up the pen. "The police would just laugh in our face and send us straight back here if they don't lock us up and throw away the key."

She circled a name and Emily felt a shiver of relief.

"The police won't lock you up," she said in a firm voice. "I won't let them."

Gladys circled another name, then another.

Three names.

Three dead boys in the ground.

Emily reached out to pick the pages up, then paused as Gladys slowly drew another circle on the paper. And another. And another.

Until the dive into disappointment took her breath away, Emily hadn't realised how much she'd been hoping for a miracle from this woman. Was that why she'd pushed this visit all the way to the end of the day, despite being easily able to get out of her earlier obligations? She hadn't wanted to be left in the doldrums with no rope available to pull her out?

"You mustn't tell on me," Gladys said, returning the paper and pen.

Emily made a big deal of putting it away in her purse just so she wouldn't have to meet the woman's eyes. She didn't want her dip into depression to scare her.

"Did the man find the axe?" the elderly woman asked, grabbing hold of Emily's hand and crushing it until her bones shrieked in pain. "I saw him digging out there. Did he find it?"

"The man was fixing the plumbing," Emily explained, extricating herself from Gladys's tight grasp with force. "He had to dig up the pipe to repair it, but the water flow is back to normal."

Gladys frowned, placing her trembling fingertips up to her temple. "But he cut the man down?" She stared down at the floor, shaking her head. "No, no. He cut the tree down. The oak?"

"The tree is still out there. I'm sure if it needs to be cut down, Allain will organise it."

"Not Allain, the other one." Gladys clicked her fingers together. "Samuel." She giggled. "Samuel the animal." She held her index finger up to her lips. "But you're not allowed to say we call him that."

"I promise, I won't tell Samuel anything." Emily stood up, her thigh muscle protesting the movement and threatening to cramp once again. "Thank you for your time, Gladys."

"You can't leave," the woman said, aghast, struggling to her feet and running to the door. "Nurse!" She turned back to Emily, digging her fingers hard into her shoulder, her breath fetid and warm against her cheek.

"They'll never let you leave."

CHAPTER ELEVEN

For once, Emily was glad to see Rebecca's unsmiling face. While the nurse coaxed Gladys into bed, she kicked the door shut leaving Emily outside in the corridor.

The spurt in adrenaline as a result of the elderly woman's grip and muttered threats made Emily's legs feel shakier than usual. As she walked through the interconnecting corridors, hoping to make it back to a recognisable location, she ran her hand against the wall for support.

"There you go," Crystal said in a cheerful voice when she made it to Agnes's room. "We were just about to give up on you."

As Emily walked further inside, collapsing into the chair, the medium leaned forward, her face twisting with concern.

"What happened? You look dreadful."

"Don't tell her that," Agnes scolded. "You look perfectly fine, dear. Just like you've had a bit of a shock."

Emily nodded and let the two women fuss over her, even Maude joining in by rubbing against her ankles.

"I'm okay," she said after a few minutes and felt it was the truth. With her heart settling back into its normal rhythm, her temporary fright retreated into the distance. "I was just talking to Gladys, and it all got a tad weird."

"Yeah, it gets like that."

"Knock, knock," a woman's voice called out, a knuckle tap following a moment later.

Agnes opened the door on Suzanne Wilberforce, her dog Conker sitting obediently at her heel.

"Oh, goodness. I didn't realise you had company."

"The more the merrier," Agnes said in good humour, waving Suzanne inside. "Since there's so many of us, I might crack open a bottle of sherry. I've missed having a tipple and a chat in the evening since my Bertie passed on."

Emily took the drink with a grateful smile, though she'd steered clear of alcohol since her accident. Right now, her nerves were shouting louder than her common sense.

"I'm sorry if I came off a bit rude when we first met," Suzanne said, hitching herself up onto the desk. "I was scared if Allain got his knickers in a twist over Maude, he might re-examine the evidence for me keeping Conker here."

With the warm glow of sherry blooming in her stomach, Emily waved it off. "I don't know why you'd be worried. At a guess, he never bothered to look too closely when you and Conker first arrived."

"No, he didn't." Suzanne took a large gulp, draining half the small glass, and gazed at her dog with an adoring expression. "I put on my most pompous voice and fixed him with a steely gaze, like this." She narrowed her eyes and stared at Emily, who jumped.

"I wouldn't have checked anything, either," she admitted. "Right now, I feel like I've done something wrong."

The group laughed and clinked their glasses together. Maude and Conker eyed each other, then each decided the other dog was the most boring animal in the world.

"Did you get anything out of Gladys except a deep, unsettling fear?" Crystal asked when the conversation lulled. "Or was it all a bit of a goose chase?"

"She circled some names," Emily said, pulling the school roll out of her bag. "But I don't know if they mean anything. I thought for a moment, she might've been naming the victims." She jerked her head towards the window. "Except she circled far too many."

"Do you think there are more bodies out there to find?" Agnes said, her hand reaching up to massage her throat. "It's been bad enough having those graves for a view since I moved in. If it's going to be a recurring theme, I think I'd rather move to my second-choice retirement village, over in Christchurch."

"I hope not." Crystal leaned forward, tapping Emily on the shoulder. "What does your ghost say? Are there more bodies out there?"

"My ghost doesn't say anything, that's the problem." Emily flattened out the pages and handed them to the medium. "And he's not here."

Crystal frowned at the answer. "Why not? When you were dealing with that nightmare woman a few months back, she followed you around everywhere."

"She certainly did." Emily held her bottom lip between her fingers, squeezing and releasing in time with her pulse. "I don't really know. I suppose I didn't invite him and he's not really quick on the uptake if you get what I mean."

"Well, I hope you remember to next time." Crystal was smiling but Emily ignored that, focused instead on the chastisement in her words.

"I guess I'm being an awful host."

"Ha. What about me?" Agnes held her glass out, giggling. "I refilled my own glass and didn't even bother to ask if anyone else wanted a top-up."

Emily fought a brief battle with her future self and lost. "I'd love one. After the visit to the other side of the home, my nerves are on fire."

"Oh, yes." Suzanne's mouth pulled down. "I don't blame you. When we had the dementia and mental health patients mixed in and we all lived together, I never minded them in the slightest. Now Stoneybrook's stuck them all in the same place, it upsets my stomach just to walk over for a visit."

"They weren't always separate?" Surprise cut through Emily's sherry-flavoured buzz. "I just assumed the village had been set up that way."

"No. It's a new thing." Suzanne drained the last of her sherry and held her glass out to Agnes. "When I turned up two years ago, the whole place was shared with the residents who needed more care placed in rooms closer to the nurse's station."

"That sounds nicer." Agnes pulled Maude into her lap and fussed over her ears. The dog panted happily, snuffling through her turned-up nose. "I don't like the way it feels like us and them."

"Exactly. And it's harder now to get a card game together. Just because someone can't keep everything straight in their head doesn't mean they stop being able to do anything." A sad smile spread over her face while her eyes gazed into a memory. "I used to clean up at poker, I can tell you."

Suzanne shook herself and winked. "Especially when

we stopped playing for matchsticks and put some money on the table."

Agnes choked on her sherry. "You didn't!"

The woman winked and pulled a zip across her lips.

"It seems an odd decision to make." Emily turned to Crystal who was still perusing the list of names. "The move today is towards integration, not segregation. I'm surprised the managers let this decision go through."

"Managers." Suzanne snorted. "There's only Allain and his daddy's money running this show." She shook her head and tapped the side of her nose. "Or Margaret, if the truth be told. He might have left her on reception, but she definitely wears the pants in that relationship."

"They're a couple?" Emily sat back, feeling stunned under the onslaught of new information. "I never would've guessed."

"Just wait and watch them. They slip up every now and again, even though they think they're so smart and secretive."

"Do these names mean anything to you?" Crystal asked, bringing Emily back to the reason for their visit. "Billy Gibbons. Astrid Wallheimer. Maui Hilliburton. Frederick Wilmott. Aaron Matterway. Timothy Burt."

"Fred is a resident here," Suzanne said before Emily could speak. "But I don't recognise the others."

"Astrid is the name the ghost gave me, last night," Emily said. "But the others are a mystery."

Agnes frowned out the window, one of Maude's front paws in either hand. "The surname Hilliburton rings a bell, but not Maui." She frowned and danced the English Bulldog from side to side. "Aroha," she burst out a moment later, relief clear in her voice. "I used to work in the supermarket next to an Aroha Halliburton. She lived over on Tenacre Street in the green wooden house near the end."

Crystal nodded. "I know the one. How long ago are you talking about?"

"Donkey's years but a look in the phone book will soon tell you if she's still there."

"Would Maui be her husband?" Emily asked.

"No." Agnes shook her head and dropped Maude's paw to pick up her sherry again. "She was unmarried. Batted for the other team and never wound up with anyone permanent. It might be a brother."

"What about the others?" Crystal stared around the group, then sighed when nobody spoke up. "This is such a dreadful business, I'm starting to believe we're better off leaving it all to the police. We should drop this into them on the way home."

"That's an easy suggestion when you're not the one with a man in your room." Emily shifted in her seat. The room felt stifling. "I'm not waiting around for Sergeant Winchester to sort this out. He's had decades to do that and couldn't even find the bodies."

And I don't want to see the expression he showed me last night, ever again.

Emily could feel the other women exchanging glances but was too tired to care. "The names probably don't mean anything. Gladys just seemed lost within her own mind. The only thing she volunteered was about how she wanted to take an axe and cut down the oak tree."

"We could try asking the head nurse to sit in," Suzanne said. "Rebecca's been working at Stoneybrook for all the time I've been here. She probably knows Gladys better than anyone."

The suggestion rankled Emily. "I'm not asking that

woman to do anything of the sort. Gladys thinks she's keeping her prisoner, with good reason."

Suzanne raised her eyebrows but didn't add anything.

"Well, this party's turned into a downer," Crystal said with a laugh. "I vote we head home for the evening. If anyone thinks of some bright ideas of how to proceed, let us know."

"I'm sorry," Emily whispered to Agnes as she patted Maude goodbye. "I didn't mean to upset anybody."

Agnes rolled her eyes. "It's the unidentified bodies in the back yard that are upsetting me. Your bad mood because you have a ghost giving you a taste of hashtag metoo is nothing on top of that." She waved her hand out to the courtyard where the holes grew in the gathering shadows. "They're the ones who keep me up at night."

Emily stared into the darkening gloom. The PC she'd seen earlier patrolled the perimeter of the tape. Soon, he'd need a torch to find his way.

"I wish my ghost was more forthcoming." With an extra pat on Maude's head for good luck, Emily adjusted her handbag and joined Crystal by the door. "I'll keep you in the loop if he does decide to talk."

As she and Crystal walked past reception, a woman banged on the counter. Margaret had left while they were with Agnes and the night porter Erik flushed at the action.

"I want to visit with my father, and I don't care if it's after seven. It's not as though he'll be asleep. He only gets a few hours a night."

"We can't let you go to his room without a prior appointment," Erik said, his eyes focused on a point midway between him and the woman. Judging from his expression, he'd recited the rule a few times already.

"This is nonsense." The woman slammed her fist down

on the countertop again. "This is his home and I want to pay him a visit. It's not a hospital or a prison on lock-down. I shouldn't have to make an appointment to visit my father in his own home!"

Erik turned at the sound of Crystal and Emily's shuffling footsteps, hope written large across his face. "Evening, ladies."

"Why isn't she allowed to visit?" Emily asked, dropping her own baggage to pick up a stranger's. "Unless her father's specifically asked her not to, shouldn't the family be allowed at any time?"

"I'm just letting you know the rules," Erik said, holding one hand up as a shield. "If you want to visit anybody in the rear units, you must have an appointment."

"But why?" Emily leaned her elbows on the counter, easing the full weight off her feet. "It's not as though she's throwing a loud party. After seven isn't the witching hour."

"You might disturb other residents."

"That applies to anybody living here and having people to visit. Why's there a different set of rules for the people in the back half of the building?"

"Because they're..." Erik's lips contorted as his mouth struggled to find the right word.

"You think because my dad has trouble remembering things, he won't want his daughter to pop in and say hello?"

"I'd have thought it would be beneficial for him." Emily tapped her forefinger on the counter. "Surely, he'll feel worse off if he can't see his daughter?"

As Erik's hand crept up to pull at his earlobe, Emily took matters into her own hands. She turned to the woman and asked, "Why don't we just go down there and see if he minds you stopping in? If he asks you to leave, I guess you should go but if not..." She shrugged.

They rushed away from the desk. Emily resisted the urge to glance back but Crystal felt no such compunction. "Ha! The man's pretending we weren't even there."

"Thank you for stepping in." The woman extended a hand. "My name's Jane Warren."

"Nice to meet you. What room's your dad in?"

"I don't remember the number. It's third along the hallway on the right-hand side past the nurse's station."

Crystal tugged on Emily's arm. "Hold up. Looks like more trouble."

Nurse Rebecca stood at the end of the corridor with her arms folded across her chest. "You don't have an appointment and it's too late to visit."

Emily guessed Erik hadn't ignored them after all, just passed the buck.

"Go on," she told Jane. "Knock on your dad's door while I speak to the nurse."

Rebecca frowned, but when Jane walked straight at her, she stepped to one side, letting the woman go past.

"I have a few questions about how you run things over here," Emily said, stepping right up to the woman. "For starters, why do you insist that poor woman needs to make an appointment just to visit her dad?"

"You don't understand the amount of attention some of my residents require," the nurse replied, her lip curling. "It's for the benefit of the family members that we have fair warning. I don't know about you, but I'd rather not see my loved ones soiling themselves, or in such a state they think I'm trying to kill them."

A memory flashed into Emily's mind. Christchurch Hospital, after her car accident. She saw her fingers digging into the neck of her supposed best friend while inside she raged.

Emily shook her head, dismissing the memory while the understanding remained. "Surely, not every member of Stoneybrook requires that level of planning."

"For those that don't, we won't ask for appointments." Nurse Rebecca sighed, dropping her arms down to her side. "We go through this in detail when a resident's status deteriorates." She jerked her head toward the room Jane had disappeared inside. "We've been through this discussion with Ms Warren before."

On less sure ground now, Emily eased her weight onto her back foot. "You locked Gladys into her room."

"She said she was going to bed." The nurse pulled some loose strands of hair behind her ear. "She sleepwalks, and it's easier if we contain her to the one room. If she walks out into the common area during the night and wakes up, she'll scream the place down. It upsets the staff, the other residents, and most of all it upsets her. Because she recognises her room, it doesn't affect her the same to wake up in there."

The pulse of indignation that had been thrumming through Emily's veins dissipated, leaving her unsure. She chewed on the side of her thumbnail, then pointed to the exit sign. "What about that door? Surely, it should always remain unlocked."

Crystal slid a hand into the crook of Emily's elbow, pulling her away. "Why don't we talk this over another day. When we're not all so tired and upset with everything that's happening outside."

Nurse Rebecca acted as though she hadn't heard her. "The door is locked so nobody wanders outside and gets lost. Can you imagine what it would be like to walk out the door, then lose the sense of who you are? We have residents who sometimes can't find their way from the common lounge to their bedrooms."

Emily swallowed hard, her throat clicking in the sudden silence.

"Imagine if a resident walked outside and away from the only people who know them. Losing their memories with every step until their minds are blank. Unable to tell anybody their name or where they belong. They'd be scared. Alone. Lost."

This time when Crystal tugged her arm, it was hard enough for Emily to take a few steps backwards. Her eyes stayed locked on the nurse's face. The empathy of panic narrowed her throat.

Nurse Rebecca's face crumpled with distress. "If a resident walked out an unlocked exit, they might never get back home."

CHAPTER TWELVE

*E*ven Crystal was silent as they put distance between themselves and Stoneybrook Acres. Her normal cheer could withstand a lot but not the multitude of blows delivered by their visit.

When Emily said she'd walk her to the door, Crystal waved away the offer. "Don't be silly, then you'd be alone on the way back. If an opportunistic criminal is passing by, he's just as likely to target you as me.

Halfway home, Emily veered a few streets off target and parked outside the police station. Although her earlier words were true, and she didn't trust Sergeant Winchester to solve the case anytime soon, she also wasn't about to withhold information.

Even if that information made the policeman look at her askance.

She only got as far as saying, "I've got some—" before a raised hand stopped her going any further.

The Sergeant and PC Mitchell had been bent over a computer on the desk and Emily now heard a small crackle and whispered voice come out of the speakers. Tilting her head, she picked up a few phrases amongst the static.

"—want to report a missing—"

"—left a few hours ago—"

"—from Stoneybrook Acres—"

"—gone for hours!"

"We need to get it louder," Sergeant Winchester said, throwing the task over to Officer Mitchell and turning his attention toward Emily. "Now, what can we help you with?"

She pulled out the sheaf of papers taken from the printer at Stoneybrook the night before. "Here's the printout Erik prepared for you last night." Emily tried a small smile on for size, but tiredness soon thwarted the effort.

When the sergeant continued to gaze at her, confused, she added, "When you asked about the information on file. This is what he printed out from their computer system. I picked it up and popped it into my handbag when Margaret came in."

Winchester nodded. "About Frederick Wilmott," he said. "The resident who turned out not to be missing."

Emily's face grew warm, but she persevered. Once this task was over, she could go home and straight to bed. The sherry might have given her a glow, but it was transforming into a headache. "I've also got a school roll from Oakhaven, the place Stoneybrook Acres was before they turned it into a home. Gladys Angel and Frederick Wilmott attended at the same time, and she circled some other names."

He pulled the page closer, reading down the list, then raised his eyebrows. "I don't understand. What's this got to do with the case?"

"I don't know." Emily was suddenly close to tears.

"They're just names. They might mean something or nothing. I just don't know."

The sergeant's expression changed to one of alarm as a tear slipped down Emily's cheek. She brushed it away, fighting to keep more from falling.

PC Mitchell cleared his throat and nodded to his superior. "I think I've got it worked out if you want me to play it again. I still don't know how we're meant to identify the anonymous caller though. If the responder couldn't do it at the time…"

"It didn't mean anything to the department six months ago," the sergeant said. "We didn't know there was a body buried in the back garden then." Relief crossed his face as he turned away from Emily. "Let's give it a shot."

The junior officer pressed play and Emily jumped as the static hissed through the speakers. She finally clicked to what she was listening to as an emergency operator came on the line.

"111 emergency. Do you require police, fire, or ambulance?"

"Police." The voice was high and reedy, threaded with fear even in that one word.

"You've reached the New Zealand Police Department. What's your emergency?"

"I need to report a missing person. We've had a resident walk off the property, and he hasn't returned." There was a short break, punctuated with a wavering hiss, then the voice came back on the line. Frantic. "His name is Frederick Wilmott, and he's suffering from Alzheimer's. I'm scared something bad has happened to him and he doesn't know how to find his way home."

As the responder fired a list of questions at the caller, the blood drained from Emily's face. Perhaps if she hadn't heard the woman saying virtually the same words within the hour, it wouldn't have clicked, but now she was certain.

"That's Nurse Rebecca from Stoneybrook Acres."

BACK AT HOME, an hour later, Emily stared at the male ghost from what should have been the comfort of her bed. Unfortunately, it was a lot less pleasant when accompanied by the old man's intense scrutiny.

"Wouldn't you rather sit in the lounge?" Emily asked, her voice breaking from the strain. She'd tried to ignore him for twenty minutes, and just wound herself into a state. "I can turn on the television and you can watch cartoons all night. Doesn't that sound far more interesting than staring at me?"

Apparently not.

Emily gave a huff and got out of bed, taking a pillow and the bedspread and walking through to the lounge. If he wouldn't shift from her bedroom, then she'd rather spend a lousy night asleep on the sofa than awake in her bed.

After ten minutes, her hip was whispering to her that this was a bad idea. Emily tried to turn over, nearly fell onto the floor, and finally manoeuvred to face inward. With her eyes closed, she could sense the presence of the seat back just a few centimetres away and her chest tightened. Another few minutes and her left hip added to the whispered complaints of the first.

"For goodness' sake!" Emily turned back over, facing out into the room. The male ghost was an inch away from her face, staring, and she screamed.

"Honestly, Scarface. You make enough noise to wake

the dead." Cynthia strolled into the lounge, not bothering to use the door—just straight through the wall.

"Not you, too." Emily covered her face and swallowed hard to try to keep from crying. Another scream would be a welcome relief if it wasn't for her neighbours. "Can't you both just go away and let me rest?"

"Come on, big boy. That's our marching orders." Cynthia hooked her arm through the crouching man and dragged him toward the wall. "There's a love seat out here in the back garden that I'm willing to share with you, so long as you don't get handsy."

For a moment, Emily could scarcely believe her luck. Then she scrambled back to bed to fall asleep before the situation could devolve.

To lie in her bed without anyone else in the room? Heaven.

Before she knew it, the sun shining through the window woke Emily and she cracked an eye open to check if she was still alone.

No such luck. Her silent companion sat with his back propped against the wall, staring blankly at his hands.

"I don't suppose you've regained your voice while I was asleep?" Emily asked, pulling down her nighty before flipping back the covers. "You've made me curious what you'll sound like if you ever get around to speaking."

While she fixed breakfast, Emily thought of the day ahead. Last night, Sergeant Winchester had insisted she should accompany him along to Stoneybrook Acres so she could make a formal recognition of the nurse's voice.

"Can't you do that for yourself?" she'd asked to no avail.

"We'll need you as a backup. If neither one of us can hear the similarities you can, then a witness to both will come in handy."

"At this rate, I'll have moved into Stoneybrook by stealth," she complained to Peanut who was padding her lap with his paws. "Good luck trying to make me comfortable, little fella. I've got far too many hard angles to be your pillow."

At least the sergeant was prompt. He stood beside his vehicle when Emily pulled up outside the home. She'd insisted on driving herself so she could take off to work when they'd finished. Friday was always a bonanza of donation boxes at the charity shop and she didn't want to leave Pete to have to deal with that alone.

Gregory's there, remember? He can handle the drop-offs much better than you!

"This place gives me the creeps," Emily muttered under her breath as they walked through the reception area.

"Not where I hope I end up," the sergeant agreed, and Emily coloured. She hadn't thought she'd spoken loudly enough to be heard.

"What does this report matter?"

The sergeant glanced down at Emily in surprise. "Well..."

"It's not as though Mr Wilmott did wander off. Or, if he did, he made it back again okay."

The policeman sighed. "It's a lead. Someone called the police in obvious distress around the same time a body was buried in the garden. Even if the person wasn't who they thought it was—"

"Nurse Rebecca isn't the sort to make a mistake in identification."

"Nevertheless, a call was made. Someone was missing." In a smaller voice, he added, "We don't have a lot of leads to go on, right now. The pathologist hasn't been able to identify the body from existing records. If we can't get somebody around here to admit who it is, we're looking at a man remaining unidentified and unclaimed by his family for months, if not years."

The ghost appeared beside Emily, who managed not to jump. He reached out, as though to take her hand, and looked on in despair when it travelled straight through her.

"Do you want to wait in the lounge area while I talk with the nurse?" The sergeant waved his hand at the common room. "I'll come and get you if we need anything."

Emily shuffled into the room, keeping her back against the wall. Even the ghost beside her looked terrified. After a few minutes with no one accosting her, she relaxed enough to cross the room and claim a chair.

"Hey," a familiar voice said from behind her. "Can't stay away, I see."

She turned and a jolt of pleasure ran through her as she saw the smiling face of Mr Wilmott. Emily couldn't stop herself from smiling back. "I figure, if I hang around here long enough, they'll let me have a room for free."

"You can just take over when the next one carks it," he agreed, tipping her a wink. "Like our old mate Gladys-of-the-window. She looks about on her last legs."

"Nah." Emily clenched her hands together in her lap, worried about the appropriateness of the banter but not enough to stop. "Ladies live longer than men. I'd rather put my money on you."

"You'd have a job and a half ahead of you in that case." He held his nose. "You'll be airing out that tiny box for the next three years."

"Why?" Emily stared at him, horrified. "What do you do in there?"

He pressed a hand to his chest. "I would never burden a lady with the truth of that. How about old Wilbur over there?" He jerked his head at an old man playing a game of solitaire. "Hey, Wilbur!" The man turned around. "Didn't you say the other day, you were feeling chest pains?"

The old man nodded and squeezed his left arm before turning back to his cards.

"Shouldn't he tell that to the nurse?"

"Nah. Rebecca's a good sort unless she's in a mood, but if he told her she'd have to do something." Mr Wilmott lowered his voice and leaned closer—his breath smelling of cool mints. "We try very hard to keep a policy of DNR around here." He tapped the side of his nose. "Unofficially, since our families have the medical powers of attorney, for the most part."

Emily sat back, unable to tell if he was joking. Before she could say anything, Sergeant Winchester beckoned her from the doorway.

"What's he doing here?" Mr Wilmott asked, a sharp edge to his voice.

"We think Rebecca called the police around the time the body was buried under the patio." Emily stood up, easing out her back until her spine popped. "He thinks it might be a lead."

A pallor stole over Mr Wilmott's face, then he stood up and moved away. Emily shrugged and joined the sergeant by the door.

"Don't worry," he said by way of greeting. "It's not rocket science. Just listen to Rebecca as she reads out the script I've given her, then make the ID."

Emily folded her arms across her body, giving herself a small hug. "Didn't you recognise her voice, then?"

"No. And you'll hear why in a minute."

His lips were set in a grim line as he walked ahead of her into the nurse's office. The smell of antiseptic and menthol greeted her, the chemicals setting Emily's teeth on edge.

"Good morning," Nurse Rebecca said in a voice heavy with a cold. "I really think this is ridiculous."

"We'll be out of your hair in a second. I'll just get you to speak the words I've written down there."

Rebecca stared at Emily for a long minute, then dropped her eyes and coughed. "Sorry," she said as the burst came to a halt. "I've developed a cold. One of the disadvantages of working here."

"Shouldn't you take the day off?" Emily asked, sure the nurse was faking but willing to play along. "If you pass that infection on to the residents, it could turn out a lot worse for them."

The nurse's lip curled. "I was just clearing up a few things and was about to do that when you showed up."

"Why don't we stick to the point of our visit?" Sergeant Winchester rapped his knuckles on the desk. "Could you recite the lines, please?"

"I'm getting to it." Rebecca raised a hand to her neck. "My throat is very dry and sore."

The sergeant sighed, rubbing his fingers over his eyebrows until the hairs stuck out at odd angles. "Okay. We don't want you to be uncomfortable. Why don't you have a glass of water and then we'll start?"

Emily crossed her eyes but only while she was staring down at her lap, so no one saw. The boxes would be piling up outside the back door of the shop right now. Poor Pete would be frantic, running between the arriving stock and guarding the till. He'd shift three boxes to every one that Gregory managed.

"Maybe we should leave it—"

Emily broke off as a scream sounded from next door.

She scrambled to her feet, heart pounding, and ran into the room.

Gladys was pounding her fists on the window, but the noise didn't come from her. The ghost stood back, an unearthly sound still emerging from his throat, pointing outside.

"What is it?" Emily yelled at him, already knowing he wouldn't answer. She ran to Gladys's side instead, standing on tiptoes to get a better view over the woman's shoulder.

Frederick Wilmott sat on a large branch in the oak tree.

A noose circled his neck.

CHAPTER THIRTEEN

Emily forgot the pain in her hips and the creeping numbness in her legs. She sprinted down the corridor. On instinct, she ignored the exit door closest, running through the retirement home corridors instead.

Her lungs burned as she reached the reception desk. A startled Margaret glanced her way and Emily pointed outside, unable to pause and speak.

PC Perry was still standing guard next to the burial sites. His head jerked up at the noise of her running, and when she pointed in frantic gestures to the tree, he saw and ran ahead.

"Don't jump," the officer yelled out as he reached the base of the tree. His palms slapped against the trunk. "Stay there. Just hold on to the branch so you don't fall."

Frederick Wilmott stared down at them, his face a study in misery. Emily struggled to fit together this new image with the jovial man she'd joked with just a few minutes before.

"Fred!" Her breath caught and Emily coughed, the pain

in her lungs triggering a fit. As soon as she could, she added, "Don't jump. We can talk about it, can't we?"

"There's nothing to talk about," he called down. A tear slipped from his eye and fell to the ground. He was leaning too far forward.

In terror, Emily found strength. She climbed up the trunk of the tree, yelling out when her hands lost purchase and gravity dumped her back on the ground. "What's happened? Why are you doing this?"

She stared at him, watching the pain fill his eyes. He leaned out, leaned out.

"No! Don't you do it. Not while we're standing here. It's not fair!"

"Go away if you don't want to see. I'm not about to stick around just to save you a bit of bother."

"Mr Wilmott." Sergeant Winchester arrived, holding his hands up in a steadying gesture at the man. "Please don't move. Let's talk about whatever's troubling you. I'm sure it's not as bad as you think. We can sort this out."

"There's nothing to be sorted. I'm sick of this place. Now move away!" Mr Wilmott flapped his arm at them, as though they were flies that could be swatted away.

"We can have a counsellor here in ten minutes," the sergeant called back. "If you need to talk out your problems, they'll be able to help."

"Forget the shrink," Emily said, exasperated. "We need a ladder. How did you even get up there? Are you Superman?"

Frederick chuckled, then bit the sound off. "Go back inside. I don't want to kick any of you while I'm struggling."

"Do you even hear yourself?" Emily thumped her hand against the trunk of the tree. "If you want to top yourself, why not take a handful of pills and drift off to sleep? This is no way to do it.”

“Pills take time, love. I don't have time.”

“Why? What do you think is happening to the afterlife that you're in such a hurry?” Emily turned, searching for the ghost, but he was nowhere in sight. “I've heard of FOMO before but that's ridiculous.”

He chuckled again. “Listen to you. The old lady's down with the lingo, eh?”

“This isn't a joke. I've probably strained my hips coming out here at a sprint. Now get down!”

Instead, Frederick leaned back, lining his body up with the thick branch so Emily could barely see his face. “No,” he said and sighed. “It's not a joke, love. I've been living on borrowed time for too long as it is.” Another tear fell, his moods swinging wildly. “Rebecca didn't have anything to do with this. I hope you remember that.”

“You murdered that man.” Emily spoke the words in a monotone statement. Her mind was whirling with the possibilities, tying together the strings of evidence. “Who was he?”

Frederick shook his head. “It's too late. I've acted too badly.” He was crying openly now. “Even if I didn't do it myself, I should never have let Allain and Margaret talk me into this.”

“Talk you into what?” Emily took a step back to see him better. “What are you going on about?”

“I've been pretending to be someone I'm not.” The man sighed. “And all the while I was acting, the real Frederick Wilmott was out dying. If only I'd spoken up sooner, I might have saved the man's life.”

A cold chill worked its way from the soles of Emily's

feet all the way up to the nape of her neck. The ghost stood beside her, his eyes pleading.

"If you're not Frederick Wilmott, who are you?"

"I'm Michael Tosh. Originally of Saint Manning, then Christchurch, and now Pinetar. For the past six months, I've been living a lie." He shook his head, eyes brimming with fresh tears. "I can't do it anymore."

Sergeant Winchester moved until he was positioned directly underneath Michael. "Can you confirm the body of the adult male found in these grounds was that of Frederick Wilmott?"

The ghost turned toward the officer, nodding his head. He gave a single hoot, then returned his attention to the man in the tree.

"I don't know," Michael said. "By the time I arrived, he was either long gone or long dead."

"But why have you been impersonating him?" Emily called out. "I don't understand."

"For my part, it was to get food in my belly and a roof over my head. The few months before I moved in here, I was living out of my car."

The sergeant glanced around the small group. There were two people notably absent. "And you're saying that Allain Homeaway and Margaret Tillerson asked you to pretend to be Mr Wilmott?"

"Yeah." Michael sobbed. "It's such a dreadful thing, I can't ever take it back. If he was here right now..."

"What would you say?" Emily glanced at the ghost by her side, then turned back to Michael. "If you're correct, then he was dead by the time you turned up on the doorstep."

"But I stopped anyone finding that out, didn't I? I took the hot food and the warm room, and I justified it to myself by saying that a winter living out of my car would have killed me."

"You should never apologise for saving your own life." Emily shielded her face with one hand as the sun crept higher in the sky. "And haven't you already tried to make amends? You've befriended the men and women who live beside you when many couldn't be bothered. Who's going to talk to them or listen to their health complaints if you jump and end it all?"

"I stopped the police being able to find the killer!" Michael gripped hold of the branch with both hands, his knuckles straining to white. "If it weren't for me—"

"I don't think you need worry on that account," Sergeant Winchester said in a low rumble. "I've got a fair idea where we need to look."

"Wouldn't you rather make up for things here and now?" Emily swallowed hard, trying to think of something more to add. "Surely, it's better to do some good while you're on this earth than jump and leave everything just the same?"

Michael didn't answer. His eyes stared fixedly into the middle distance, ignoring everyone standing below.

"Poor Gladys is glued to the window," Emily said, pointing back to the home. "Is this a sight you really want her to see?"

The man jerked upright, his eyes now travelling to the far-off room where a familiar silhouette stood, palms still banging on the glass. "What? No. You need to get back there and move her away."

"You want her to move, ask her yourself!" Emily looked at the ghost to her side, drawing strength from his silent presence. "She's already distraught. It was her screaming that let us all know you were out here."

"But I didn't..."

"Come down now, hey?" the sergeant said. "We'll sort things out as best we can and assign as much blame as you can bear."

Emily thought those words would tip the man over the edge, but Michael nodded in relief. He shuffled back to the main trunk of the tree and swung himself down, showing the dexterity of a man half his age.

Only when his feet were touching solid ground did her chest loosen enough to inhale a large gulp of air.

"PC Mitchell?" Sergeant Winchester turned to the younger officer. "How about you put a call through for backup? When another patrol car is on its way, I'd like you to arrest Allain and Margaret for perverting the course of justice."

The officer's chest puffed out as he nodded, then jogged back to the building.

"I'll take you down to the station," the sergeant said, putting a hand on Michael's upper arm. "Once you and Nurse Rebecca have answered some questions, we might even be able to bail you back here for the night."

Once the sergeant had deposited the still sobbing man in the back seat of his car, he walked through to the nurse's station. Rebecca sat at the desk, head in her hands. To Emily, she looked fully aware of what was coming.

But Sergeant Winchester held back for a second. "Could you please tell me who Frederick Wilmott was?"

The nurse glanced up, her eyes bloodshot. "He was a resident here, and a patient." She smoothed her hair back from her brow and gazed at Emily. "You asked me why we keep the exit door locked, he's why. He suffered from Alzheimer's and liked to sit out in the garden. One day, he wandered away from his usual spot and never came back."

"How could you just let them cover it up?" Emily asked. She pressed a hand against her belly, feeling the vibrations of her stomach churning.

Rebecca sighed. "Because if I told anybody, I'd lose my job. We all knew by midnight on the first night, he was dead and gone. The temperatures outside were freezing, and he was an old man, not dressed for the weather."

"You put this career above the life of a person under your care?"

"Don't judge me." The nurse stood up, straightening her back. "If I lost my job here, even for a few days, all the residents here would be in danger. Allain Homeaway would never pay the rates required to get a decent replacement. Half the staff on duty here barely speak English and don't have more than a carer's certificate. If you knew how many times a day I have to stop someone administering medication at the wrong dose, it'd scare the life out of you."

Emily put her hands on her hips. "But, surely a doctor—"

"There's no doctor on staff. We have a GP come in once a month to address any complaints. It's not often enough, and it leaves me in charge of administering the medication to this entire facility."

The sergeant shook his head. "Why didn't you call the police? If there was an active investigation—"

"I did call. Why didn't you follow up?" She glared at the officer. "Nobody from your station even bothered to come out here to check. Did somebody even phone?"

Sergeant Winchester pulled at his collar. "We have a call on file. An officer spoke to Allain Homeaway who insisted all his residents were accounted for."

"Great job, Sergeant. Heaven forbid you spend half an hour coming down here to check."

"We also patched a call through to the ministry of health. They performed their bi-annual appraisal early and reported back the same."

"I'm so glad your conscience is clear."

Winchester pulled a face. "What difference would it have made? If we came down here, it would've been exactly the same story. Unless somebody came forward—"

"Allain and Margaret pulled this charade together in an afternoon. There's no way it would've stood up to scrutiny. The other residents would have known Michael wasn't who he said he was. It took them two full days to organise the room changes to reduce the chance of someone noticing. You saw Michael—the guilt's been eating him alive right from the very start. He would've told you everything a few minutes after you got here if you'd only come."

She sat back down, her face crumpling in distress. "Why didn't you come?"

*L*ater that afternoon, Emily was sorting through the new donations at the charity shop when Crystal dropped in to see her.

"I don't suppose you feel up to wielding a box-cutter, do you?" Emily asked as her friend popped a beaming face through the door. "If I don't get a hurry-on with these, I'll be in here tomorrow and Sunday."

"Give me a reason and I'm happy to cut anything up."

"I don't think I want to delve into that statement!"

They worked alongside each other for a few minutes, Crystal humming a psalm beneath her breath. As the pile came into shape, Emily sat back on her heels. "Did you drop by for a reason?"

"Just to gossip," Crystal said, tapping the side of her nose. "A little birdie told me there were a few arrests down at Stoneybrook Acres today."

"Yes, there were, and not before time." Emily pulled down the sleeve of her blouse to rub it across her forehead where her exertion had produced a light sheen of sweat. "The director and the receptionist."

"Ah. I wondered if they were having a relationship." Crystal nodded, seeming content, and lasted a full minute before further enquiring, "Your new ghost friend has gone, then?"

Emily glanced into the corner where he stood, swaying back and forth as usual. Why he didn't sit down, she couldn't fathom. It made her knees swell just to look at him.

"I take it that's a no." Crystal slid the blade of the box cutter along the masking tape on her current box, a smile appearing as she reached the end and opened up the flaps. "Ugh." She folded the cardboard back over. "Unless there's a market for old men's magazines, I think you should steer clear."

"There is and I won't, not if the charity can earn some money from them." Still, Emily wasn't in any hurry to take a look. There was an enormous difference between second-hand and soiled and she'd rather wait till she had gloves.

"I did hear a rumour around town that Allain denies any part in your ghost's murder," Crystal said, flexing her hand before wielding the box cutter again.

"Already?" Emily asked with a smile. She'd returned to Pinetar after a long absence just a few months ago and the speed of gossip in a small town still amazed her. It had only been a few hours since the arrest, yet already speculation had circled.

"Apparently, they truly believed he walked away from the home and lost his way back."

"Not that it's any better," Emily said, her hands curling into fists. "Not reporting a missing person when you think he can't find his way back home?" She shook her head. "It's unconscionable. At least Michael had a reason for doing what he did, although Allain and Margaret taking advantage of a man who's fallen on hard times just makes everything worse, yet again."

"Well, not quite as bad as murder."

"If they thought Mr Wilmott was out there, scared and alone, it is. To let someone die through fear you'll lose your business is just as bad as wielding a knife or a rope to kill the person directly. Plus, Allain was cutting corners. Nurse Rebecca was scared to leave the home because he wouldn't employ adequately trained staff."

Crystal raised her eyebrows at that, and Emily flushed a little. Yes, she had taken an adverse stance against the woman on short acquaintance and had to accept she'd judged her too harshly.

"If they'd just reported him missing to the police, everything would've been so different."

"It seems Stoneybrook already had a couple of black marks against it," Crystal said in a musing tone. "I think the two of them must've panicked. A third incident and the facility would go under supervision. Nobody wants to move into that sort of place. Whether the ministry closed them down or not, the business would have gone down the gurgler."

"And good riddance."

But Crystal shook her head. "Look, I don't agree for a second with what those two did, covering up your ghost's disappearance, but it'll be a sad thing if our town does lose that retirement village. Our population isn't getting any younger and I don't want to move to another city when I can't take care of myself any longer."

With that possibility on the cards for her a lot sooner than her friend, Emily conceded the point. "Not that it excuses anything."

"Of course, not. I hope they get it back up and running though. There were a lot of plans for expansion on the cards."

The two of them continued with their work, clearing up half of the boxes

"Oh." Crystal sat back, pointing the box cutter at Emily. "I almost forgot what I really came to tell you. I tracked down Aroha and it turns out Maui is her brother. He's alive and well and living just up the road in Ashburton."

While the medium appeared pleased with herself, Emily shook her head. She couldn't place the name at all.

"Much good you are at all this investigation stuff," Crystal scoffed. "It's one of the names on the list, remember? The ones that Gladys circled from the Oakhaven School roll."

Emily tipped her head forward as the memory slipped into place. "I'm not sure it'll be any help."

Crystal dismissed the sentiment with a wave of her hand. "No one ever knows if someone's going to be helpful until they hear them out. Besides, since your friend hasn't found his doorway of light through to the next realm, it can't hurt to try another avenue."

"I wish he'd just tell me what it is he wants."

"He probably wants you to stop talking about him like he's not in the room." The medium scrutinised her for a second. "You never acted this way with Cynthia."

"No, you're right." Emily sighed. "I'm being rude."

Crystal wrinkled her nose. "Well, rude-adjacent, anyway."

"Did you want me to give Maui a call and see if we can drop by and interrogate him about old times?"

"Already done. We can visit any time tomorrow." Crystal sat back and pulled an old enamel-coated canister out of her current box. It was coloured pastel blue and painted with a spray of yellow and white flowers. "This looks exactly like the set my Nana used to have."

Emily caught the tone of nostalgia in her voice. A quick appraisal told her they were worth twenty dollars snuck into the till. "Take them. It's on the house."

"I couldn't do that." Despite the words, Crystal didn't put the canister back into the box, either.

"Of course, you can. My treat. I'm aware I've been a bit of a trial recently."

"Go on, you're fine."

"No, I'm not." Emily gave a low laugh. "I'm tired all the time because this fella keeps staring at me when I'm trying to sleep. It makes me grumpy all day long and since you're the one I spend the most time with, you beat the brunt of it."

"Okay, then. Talk me into it." Crystal set the tin to one side, then resumed her search. "I don't know how you tell what's rubbish and what's gold in this lot. Most of it looks dire."

"Years of practice at knick-knack collecting, all of it gone when I downsized to my current place."

Not only due to lack of room but also for the money Emily could realise. If she'd known the objects it took her so long to obtain would be missed so little, she might have given them up earlier.

"Once we get through that one, I think we might call it a day. I'm just going to pop downstairs to the little girl's room."

She stopped by the till on the way past, giving Pete a twenty to cover Crystal's present.

"I heard you were involved in a bit of excitement up at Stoneybrook today," he said with a grin.

Emily rolled her eyes. Small town gossip. It was a wonder any bodies could remain buried with the number of tongues wagging non-stop.

Cynthia greeted Emily at the door when she arrived home. "Please tell me you've worked out how to get rid of your new friend. He's been moping around for hours, now. It gets tiring just looking at him."

"Hopefully, we'll find out something more tomorrow about the bodies of the boys found at Stoneybrook." Emily glanced into the lounge where Mr Wilmott stood, his face showing gentle despair. "We tracked down somebody in the class."

"Not that it's helped so far," Cynthia complained. "If the new one is as doolally as the rest, it'll get us nowhere."

Emily smiled at her friend's use of the word "us." Things must be dire at home during the day to refer to them as a team.

"Anyway, if you can look after Peanut tomorrow, it'll be a great help." Emily chucked the ghost cat under the chin, earning a look of pure admiration. "We could be gone for hours."

"You're taking the medium?" Cynthia gave a derisive shake of her head. "Although, I suppose since this one's alive, it'll fit with her skillset better." She raised her eyebrow at the cat. "How about it Peanut? Just you and me for the day. We can go haunt Nathaniel and Gregory."

"Or you could go for a nice walk and keep yourselves out of mischief." Emily glanced at the ghost of Mr Wilmott again, frowning. "Did he tell you anything about what happened today?"

She relayed the events, ending with a satisfied grin on the details of Allain Homeaway and Margaret Tillerson being arrested.

"No, he didn't tell me any of that." Cynthia sat, petting Peanut on her lap for a moment. "Hey, Fred! Did all these arrests slip your mind?"

The ghost stared blankly at the two of them, then his eyes drifted to the window and stayed there, his mouth drooping at the corners.

"I hope you take him along with you tomorrow," Cynthia said with a shake of her head. "Otherwise, he'll be a dampener on the day."

Emily was relieved to find Mr Wilmott absent from the car the next morning. Whether he'd chosen to stay with Cynthia or take himself off to haunt someone else with his sullen silence, she didn't know.

The day had dawned with a thick fog, the droplets forming a cloud so thick that they set off with the headlights turned on. As the route steered further inland, the visibility dwindled, then they drove out the end of the cloud into the brightness of a sunny day.

Late season lambs stood with their mothers, bleating about how cruel the cooling mornings were with their wool newly shorn. A crowd of bored cows chewed their cud in a field burned brown in the departing summer. Their eyes fixed on the car as it drove past, but they didn't bother to turn their heads. A couple of horses flicked their ears at hovering flies but otherwise kept their attention on each other.

"Do you have any questions prepared?" Emily asked, nerves waking up as the distance to Ashburton closed, firing off increasing rounds of anxiety. "I'm not the best when it comes to talking to total strangers."

"I thought we'd just wing it." Crystal appeared completely unfazed by the task ahead. "It's no different from holding a session with a new client. Once we have a little banter about the weather, it'll be like we're old friends."

The medium paused for a while, brow furrowed. "You know I grew up there?"

Emily shook her head, shifting in her seat to take a closer look at her friend. "No. I presumed you were from Pinetar."

"Born and raised in Ashburton. My parents used to run a small lifestyle block, not that they were called that then."

"We called those no-lifestyle blocks back in my old job," Emily said, smiling at the memory. "Not enough land to make any real money but enough work and responsibility to keep you occupied, day and night."

"That's it. Everybody in town had it much the same. I used to pester my mum and dad to let me stay at Nana's house during the school holidays. It was the only time I'd ever get to rest."

"Whereabouts did she live?"

"In Christchurch. She lived up the hill on Clifton Terrace, looking down on Sumner beach."

The longing in Crystal's voice made Emily twist toward her. If they'd been standing in conversation instead of trapped inside car seats with belts, she would have reached out.

"In Ashburton, I was always different. The kid who stood out by how she dressed and how she spoke. In and around Sumner Beach, there were lots of people just like me, including my nana. She was the one who first taught me there was more to life than just what we could see. I learned palm reading and astrology by the time I'd graduated the primers."

"Probably not the best way to help you fit in."

Crystal laughed, tears glimmering in her eyes. "Not at all. At least when I reached high school, I'd had practice at being the odd one out. When a few others drifted from the mainstream, I was there waiting."

"Leader of the freaks and geeks?"

"Something like that. It was the first time I'd had friends in a while, that's for sure."

Emily turned back to face forward, her hip sighing with relief at the posture change. "Why did you move to Pinetar instead of to Christchurch, then?"

This time, it was Crystal's turn to flick a curious glance Emily's way. "You know."

"Know what?" Emily shook her head, the conversation getting away from her.

"Pinetar is the home for all the freaks in our nation. The only people who stand out there are straight folks."

Emily opened her mouth to counter the statement, then slowly closed it again. She could hardly challenge Crystal's words with a declaration that *she* was normal. After all, she was going to meet someone she didn't know to try to rid herself of a silent ghost.

If there was a standard for normality in the world, Emily couldn't imagine her own situation rested inside it.

Before she could think of another retort, Crystal had pulled the car to the side of the road, nudging the front bumper close to a recycling bin, emptied by the council but not yet dragged inside.

"Well, let's get in there and see what Maui has to say for himself."

Emily reached a hand out, to hold Crystal back for a minute, but she was too slow. The door slammed.

As she joined the medium on the doorstep, Emily swallowed hard then jumped. The ghost had joined them, after all, standing behind Crystal with his hands hanging loosely by his sides. His eyes stared ahead blankly, absorbing the shadows out of the day.

CHAPTER FIFTEEN

"I haven't thought of that place in a long time," Maui Hilliburton said. From his tone, Emily gathered he didn't want to think about it now.

"Thanks for agreeing to see us," she said. "Especially on such short notice."

"It's not like I was doing anything else."

For a man in his early seventies, Maui was sprightly. He was overweight, maybe even obese by today's standards, but his joints didn't appear to have noticed. His movements were full of grace, his voice melodic.

Emily felt like a hundred years old standing next to him.

"There's tea and coffee in the kitchen if you want some," Maui said after they'd all taken a seat in his drawing room. "I won't offer to make it for you, but if you're happy to sort it, help yourselves."

"Thank you," Crystal said, abandoning Emily on the couch in order to make herself a cup of coffee.

With her bantering companion absent, Emily stared down at the carpet for a minute, then glanced at Maui with an awkward smile.

He returned it with one of his own. "You want to know about Oakhaven School, is that right?"

She nodded, clearing her throat as a test before speaking. "The police found the body of Frederick Wilmott buried on the grounds, and we wondered if you remember him from school."

"You're not with the police." Maui's voice was flat, a statement not a question.

Emily shook her head.

"No offence, but why're you here instead of them?"

Crystal came back and sat down. When Emily shot her a pleading glance, she just buried her nose in the coffee cup.

Why are we here?

The ghost stood in the corner of the room. No, that wasn't right. He skulked there. He lurked. He hunkered down and laid in wait.

"A woman at the old people's home circled your name in a school roll, along with a few others. I thought it might have bearing on the circumstances. I've just helped a friend of mine move into a room that looks straight out over the burial spot."

Maui sucked in his breath and shook his head. "No wonder you want it sorted. I can't imagine having that as a view." He pointed to his own window. "Looking out on that marker is bad enough."

Emily followed his finger and saw a small white cross set up on the opposite side of the road, a small bunch of plastic flowers beneath it. Roads the length of the country were dotted with similar adornments. The sign of a life lost to the road toll.

"Who was it?"

For a second, Emily thought the man was asking who

the marker outside his window was for, then realised her mistake. "The woman's name is Gladys Angel."

Maui chewed on the side of his bottom lip. "I remember Gladys. She used to hang around with another girl, Trish or Tricia, something like that."

"Were there many girls at the school?"

"Half and half." At Emily's expression, he laughed. "I know it's not meant to be that way, but back then there were just as many girls getting into trouble as boys were." He shrugged and pulled his mouth down. "Not that the things we were doing would be considered abnormal now. I swore at a teacher and that was enough to have me packed up and shipped out. It's not much of a distance now between here and Pinetar, but back then my parents didn't have a car and buses were expensive. I didn't see my family more than once or twice a year."

"I'm so sorry." Emily scratched the back of her right hand where her skin crawled. "It must've been awful."

"I joked for a long time it was no different to those fancy Englishmen who send their kiddies off to boarding school as soon as they can read and write. It hurt, though." Maui sat back in his chair, rubbing beneath his right eye. "For ages, I thought the reason my family didn't visit was because they hated me for what I'd done."

"I'm sure that isn't true," Crystal said.

"Nobody visited anyone much at the school." Maui shifted on the seat, gripping the armrests tightly. "Anyway, the girls were there for different reasons. Flirting with boys, kissing behind the bike sheds, that sort of stuff. For the boys involved, they'd get a wink or a pat on the back, but the girls would be sent to Oakhaven, or worse."

Emily stared across at the ghost who glowered. "Who else do you remember from that time?"

Maui stared out the window again, for so long Emily was on the verge of prompting him when he finally answered. "I hung around with Freddie, Billy, Aaron, and Tim. Sometimes there'd be other lads join in a game if we were playing bull rush or rugby, but for the most part, it was just us five."

He turned his attention back to Emily and Crystal. "They were the same age as me. Considering some lads were a lot older, we needed to club together if we wanted to avoid a beating."

"Were the other lads rough?" Emily wanted to hold her hands over her ears, squeamishness abounding, but she forced her fingers to stay clasped in her lap.

"We were all rough." Maui laughed and tapped his forehead. "The lot of us were young and angry and hurt. If somebody said the wrong thing at the wrong time, we could all go off. A school full of powder kegs, it was."

Crystal pursed her lips. "Did you hang around with Astrid and Gladys as well?"

"I didn't. At that age, I didn't really understand what girls were for, not really. Freddie spent a lot of time with Astrid. They were probably the closest thing the school had to a couple, at the time."

Again, he shifted position in his chair, this time straightening up and perching on the forward edge. "There wasn't that much opportunity for anything like that. The teachers kept an eye on us all the time, and when we finished class, the monitors took over. One step out of line, and you'd end up in the box."

Emily didn't want to ask. Didn't need to know. She was appalled when she heard her own voice enquire, "What was that?"

"Exactly what it sounds like. The school could discipline us physically, but a lot of the lads were just as big as the teachers. The headmaster devised a cooling-off system. We were locked into a small cupboard until he felt we were apologetic enough."

Crystal jumped up and walked to the window, her elbow edging straight into the ghost, who didn't bother to move. "I can't imagine," she said, clearly picturing it in her mind.

"Those names you mentioned," Emily said, wanting desperately to move the conversation along so she could return home. Hopefully, still able to sleep at night. "Gladys circled them on the school roll as well. Do you know what happened to them?"

Maui's face turned ashen. "It was a very long time ago." With a grunt, he pulled himself up out of his seat and strode towards the kitchen. "I might fetch myself a coffee after all. This talk is making me drowsy."

"Making him jittery, more like," Crystal whispered, crossing back to her seat. "Did you see the way his legs were trembling?"

"I guess I should back off a little."

"Or charge ahead." Crystal pursed her lips squinted in thought. "If the talk upsets him, he'll become more entrenched in avoiding those parts of the conversation the longer we leave him. Repeat your question when he comes back and press him for an answer."

But when Maui came back into the room, he held a box of photographs along with his coffee. "I keep these in the top cupboard and haven't brought them down for ages," he said as he settled back in his chair. "There's a good one of Gladys if I remember rightly."

Maui's memory was spot on. He handed across a picture, the yellow tones overdeveloped to give it a golden sheen. "That was her, just before she graduated and headed off to work. The headmaster found her a spot in the local butcher's shop."

Everything about the young woman in the picture was thin and sharp. Pointed elbows, angled shoulders, and a chin like a blade. If her eyes hadn't been narrowed with suspicion, she'd have been strikingly pretty. The expression took her one notch past that point, turning her vulpine.

"How old was she?" Emily handed the photograph across to Crystal who gave a faint gasp of recognition. "Sixteen, seventeen?"

"Sixteen, I'd guess. At that age, we could get a job, but the shops still paid out at the youth rates, so we were cheap labour. Before most pay equality laws as well, so Gladys would've been on a slim wicket."

"Could she have stayed on at Oakhaven longer, if she'd wanted?"

Maui snorted. "Nobody ever wanted to, so I doubt anybody ever asked." He frowned at the next photograph. "This is the lads, all together." He turned it over and nodded. "The names are written on the back."

The picture looked similar to the one in Gladys's room, but this one missed out the girls. Either they'd already left the frame or were waiting to join. Emily showed the scribbles to Crystal.

"Freddie Wilmott, Maui Hilliburton, Billy Gibbons, Aaron Matterway, Tim Burt."

"That's us. My group."

He shuffled through a few more photographs, setting those aside. "Here's another one. This time we've got the girls in there, too."

"Astrid Wallheimer, Gladys Angel, Trish Harper."

Maui nodded. "That one must've been before Astrid

started working in the dairy after school. The headmaster Samuel lectured us all about how lazy we were in comparison." He puffed out his lips. "As if they'd let a Maori boy from the bad school work in their precious shop. I couldn't go in there to spend money without them making me turn out my pockets."

"Did she change her hair or something?"

The man stared back at Emily blankly and she blushed.

"You said it must be before she started work there. How can you tell that just by looking?"

"Oh," Maui nodded, a nostalgic smile returning to his lips. "She got fat after. Too many sweets while the store owner wasn't watching. We would've given her more stick for it, but she snuck some out for us as well."

Unlike Gladys, Astrid was a sturdier and more rounded build. Emily could easily imagine the pounds piling onto her, turning the girl into a stocky woman, ready to work the fields and bear children.

"Who took the photos?" Crystal glanced over to Maui with her usual easy smile. Emily had been around her long enough to know it hid a mind like a steel trap. "If all your friends are in them?"

"It would've been matron. She could tell you off until your ears bled if you didn't tuck the corners of your bed right in the morning, but she was a good stick." He held his hand out, and Crystal handed back the precious images with some reluctance. "She must've got them developed at the same time as some official ones. They were always getting up to line up in our best clothes, to make out the school was transforming us into little angels."

Maui stared hard at each photograph as he replaced them all in the box, lining them up so they lay flat. When he put the lid on, he brushed it with one hand, giving it a pat before he placed it on the table.

His face collapsed into sadness as he turned back to the women, tears gleaming in his eyes. "You're not here about Freddie, are you?" He gave a long sigh, his chest deflating. "I guess the police found the bodies of my mates, then."

CHAPTER SIXTEEN

After their answer, Maui fell silent for a few minutes. Emily glanced over to the ghost, still standing in the corner, silent and dreary. Crystal shifted on her seat, fidgeting and clicking a fingernail against her teeth.

"What happened?" Emily asked when the silence grew louder than she could stand. "Who hurt those boys?"

"They hurt themselves," Maui said. He wiped a hand over his forehead, his cuff absorbing the thin layer of sweat. With a grunt, he shifted his weight over to his left side and lifted the shirt up on his right.

A scar mottled the skin under his ribcage, drawing a jagged line towards his belly button, then fading away.

"I got that in the same incident where the boys died," Maui said, his voice catching. He let the shirt drop back into place, turning his face away from the women. "We all should've known better, but we were trying to do something nice."

"The oak tree?" Emily thought of Gladys's panicked voice, *cut it down. Fetch the axe. Chop the tree down.*

"Yeah, that's the one. It gave the school its name." With

a wipe over his eyes, Maui turned back to them, giving an awkward laugh. "Well, *it* didn't but the pretentious git who ran the place took the name from there."

"I saw some old cut marks in the trunk," Emily said, frowning as she brought the picture up in her mind's eye. "But it didn't go all the way through."

"No. It never came close to coming down. I don't know how much bigger it's grown over the years, but it was a serious size even way back then. One of our tasks on a Saturday during the autumn was to pick up all the acorns so they wouldn't dull the lawnmower blade when the gardener got to work."

"Like squirrels," Crystal said, wrinkling her nose. "I used to try to eat acorns just to see why they bothered to store them in all the children's books I read."

"The New Zealand squirrel." Maui shook his head. "I can tell you it's a thankless job. Even as a teen, my back would ache after an hour, bending over to pick them up from the grass. The thought of doing it now..." He trailed off, ending the words with a shudder.

Emily cleared her throat. "Who took an axe to it? Was it the gardener?"

"No. That man had more sense than the one who ran the place." Maui shook his head and took his and Crystal's cups back into the kitchen. When he returned to the drawing room, he had a box of tissues in his hand. "Just in case."

"Were you picking up acorns on the day...?" Emily didn't know enough about the incident to fill in the blanks. After a minute with no response, she tried, "On the day it happened?"

"No. It was well into winter by then. We'd stopped getting the frosts in the mornings, but the weather was bitterly cold. We had grey cloud every day for a week, so the sun didn't stand a chance."

Maui shifted in his chair again, leaning his head back and closing his eyes. "It was a Thursday—a few hours after classes ended—and we climbed up the tree to cause a distraction. Worked a treat as well since the head's office looked straight out over the grounds. We swung onto the biggest branch, probably a good six to eight feet off the ground and sat in a line."

Emily was about to ask what they were causing a distraction from, then thought better of it. Maui seemed lost in a reverie and she didn't want to break the spell. It might be the one chance she had to hear the story.

"You know how some days, even the gentlest breeze feels like it's full of sharp knives, cutting you straight to the bone? The afternoon was like that. While I was sitting in the tree, all I kept thinking about was Matron stoking the fire in the common room and how great it would be to sit in front of it."

The old man cracked open one eye and fixed it on Emily. "I used to shove my butt as close to the fire guard as I could, sometimes pressing right against it. There's a scar somewhere I'm not going to show you, with a crisscross from the iron. It got so hot after hours pressing against it, my shorts burned clean through."

He laughed and shifted position again, now staring up at the stucco ceiling. "I was more scared of what matron would do than I was worried about the pain. If I'd gone to her, she might've dunked me in some cold water before the burn set. Instead, I hid in my room and swapped out my woollen pants with my summer shorts and hoped no one would ever see it."

Crystal winced. "I'm enough of a baby when I get steam on my fingers."

"Yeah, it wasn't pleasant. Especially when it blistered. That shows you how scared I was of the rough side of Matron's tongue."

As Maui fell into silence again, Emily exchanged a glance with Crystal. The medium raised her eyebrows, jerking her head toward the man. Emily shrugged her shoulders and tilted her head.

"What happened in the tree?" Crystal finally asked, losing the battle of wills. "You said, you were all perched on a branch."

"We jeered at the headmaster. Samuel didn't like us at the best of times, and we thought having a line-up of boys sticking their tongues out and mugging him would drive him crazy. Instead, he closed the blinds to his office window so we couldn't see inside. For a long time, we thought he was just ignoring us."

Again, Crystal did the prompting. "He wasn't?"

"While we were staring at his shuttered window, he went out to the gardener's shed down the back of the school-yard and grabbed an axe. When we nudged each other, about to clamber down—it really was freezing up there and the school-issued uniform didn't come with heavy jackets—he came running. We thought he'd completely flipped his lid when he attacked the base of the tree."

"He cut it while you were still up there?" Emily's mouth gaped in horror.

"Yeah. We were far enough off the ground that we didn't want to jump, and even if we'd been low enough, who wanted to drop down and face that madman? We clung to each other and the branch. It shook with every blow of the axe."

A tear trickled down his cheek, but Maui didn't raise a hand to wipe it away. His eyes may have been fixed on the ceiling, but he appeared to be looking at something much older, happening further away.

"When the axe didn't work fast enough, Samuel jumped up and swung at our legs. Not seriously, I don't think. Looking back on it, he probably just wanted to scare us to teach us a lesson. It's hard to teach someone a lesson when you're locked up for cutting their legs off."

Emily's throat was so tight it didn't want to let her question out, but she forced it. "Did he hit any of you?"

"No. He might've nicked the sole of our shoes, but that was all." Maui's eyelid twitched, jumping in time with the pulse in his neck. "We weren't thinking clearly by that stage. We just wanted to get away. When we moved too far along the branch, it cracked at the trunk. We all fell to the ground."

Crystal gasped, though Emily felt sure she must have known which way the story was headed. "Were you hurt?"

Both Emily and Maui turned curious gazes towards the medium. After a second, she blushed and nodded. "Sorry, I got caught up and forgot."

"I was lucky," Maui continued. "Didn't even break a bone. I think I landed on top of Billy, but I'm not sure. He was next to me so if I did, he probably saved my life by breaking my fall. The ground was frozen solid. Harder than concrete."

A headache thumped at Emily's temples, a jagged line pulsing across her vision. "And the other's died?"

Maui's response was so quiet, she had to strain to pick it up. Even though the truth was obvious, she still wanted to have it confirmed.

"Why didn't you call the police?"

The man laughed, his tears now flowing freely. "I was a teenager in an institution. Do you really believe they let me have access to the phone?" He turned a pitying gaze towards her, and Emily put the pieces together.

"He locked you in the box?"

"For a few days. Matron let me out to go to the bathroom, changed my wound dressing, and fed me, then I'd go back inside. I was so stunned by what happened, I didn't put up any protest. When I was allowed back out full-time, it was hard to imagine what I thought I'd seen was even real."

"How did Freddie fit into this?" Emily leaned over and put her hand on Maui's knee. His eyes were glazing, taking him some place far away. "He wasn't in the tree?"

"We were causing a distraction so he could sneak out of the school. Astrid had left a few days before and he wanted to meet up with her."

"But he stayed?"

"The head closed his blinds. Freddie couldn't risk leaving until he knew where the man was. When he saw him heading toward the tree with the axe, he froze to the spot."

Crystal jumped to her feet, pacing to the window and back again. "But this was years ago. *Decades*. Why haven't you or Freddie told what happened in the meantime?"

"The headmaster said we'd better keep our lips buttoned if we knew what was good for us. If we didn't, if we said anything, no one would believe us. The community already had us branded as liars."

"But..." Crystal shook her head in frustration. "Surely you know that's not true."

Maui stared at her, then screwed his eyes up. "It was true, that's the problem. If it came down to believing a boy from a reform school and the headmaster, who do you think the police would side with?"

"I think they'd investigate," Emily said with a firm nod. "That's what I think."

"Because you're white. Because you're middle-aged. Because you've never been in trouble in your lives. That's not the world I lived in and it's not the world Freddie lived in either. If we'd talked to the police—if we could even get through the door—they'd have laughed in our faces. Nobody would have followed up. The entire incident was so outlandish, nobody would ever have believed what we said."

Emily opened her mouth, ready to argue again, then thought of the policemen's laughter when she first reported the murder of Mrs Pettigrew. She had advantages in life Maui could never hope to experience, but they'd still treated her like a joke.

"Yeah," she said instead, "I understand that."

"Poor Freddie was so traumatised that when Mr Leuf told him to keep his mouth shut, he took it far too seriously. I never heard him speak another word aloud in all the time he remained at the school."

Shocked, Emily turned towards the ghost. She'd never considered his muteness might be from anything other than dementia. Guilt rose in a wave of bile, burning the back of her throat.

Crystal cracked her knuckles, her face drained of all colour. "Who buried the bodies?"

"I'd guess the headmaster did it himself. I can't imagine he'd have fielded offers for help."

"But what about the other pupils?" While Emily sat back, her mind reeling, Crystal stepped closer, as though gearing up for a fight. "The school must have been full of witnesses. One or two of you—"

"Most of them were out on a school camping trip, staying at Hanmer Springs. Oakhaven went each year with another local school. A great opportunity to teach us all about nature and survival in the forest, or some such rubbish."

"Then why weren't you all there?"

"The budget didn't stretch to everyone attending every time. Since all the pupils in our year had been already, they held us back."

"Where were Gladys and Trish?" Emily sat forward, her mind processing again. "They were in your year, too, weren't they?"

"Matron had them in the kitchen. Every chance she got, she took them in there or the laundry, to learn the real skills they'd need for the future. The kitchen was on the other side of the school so they wouldn't have seen a thing."

"But... Their families." Crystal tried to mount another defence, turning her pleading face toward Emily for help.

"Do you think I'm lying?" Maui's hand curled into fists. "Is that why you turned up today? To get my story out of me so you could accuse me of fibbing about the whole thing?"

"We know nobody reported it," Emily whispered. "It's too late to think of reasons why it couldn't happen when we know for sure it did."

"It was just stupid luck that nobody else was around." Maui shook his head, the flush of red in his cheeks fading. "Although, that's probably why he started with the axe— because he knew nobody would see him."

Emily nodded. "It's pure, rotten luck."

"The head reported the boys as runaways over the next few days." Maui's voice and posture were tired, defeated.

"Since it fitted in with everyone's expectations, nobody followed up too hard. They're probably listed as missing persons still."

"Sergeant Winchester can check that out," Emily said, pushing her hair back from her face. "And I understand why you thought it would do no good to tell the police what happened before, but I think they'll be grateful if you talk to them now."

"If you want to do it today, we can give you a lift back to Pinetar," Crystal offered. "Since you've already relived it once, it might be easier to do it straight away."

Maui put his face into his hands for a moment, his shoulders shaking. Emily expected tears would be evident when he pulled them away, but his face was dry, his expression determined.

"Let's go, then," he said, standing up and stretching his spine until it popped. "Don't give me a chance to change my mind."

CHAPTER SEVENTEEN

S ergeant Winchester eyed the three of them with open suspicion as they approached the front desk of the police station. While PC Perry took some preliminary details, he pulled Emily aside.

"I hope this gets everything moving. We've had official word that a Detective Inspector from Christchurch is on his way on Monday to take over the case."

"As long as you treat Maui with respect, I'm sure he'll give you everything you need to take the case forward." Emily tipped her head to the side, observing the sheen on the sergeant's upper lip. "Did you investigate those names Gladys circled?"

He nodded, his attention moving back to the counter as PC Perry signalled him everything was finished. "Yeah. A couple of runaways and a few we couldn't trace at all." The sergeant jerked his head toward Maui. "Is he one of them?"

"Yes." Emily looked over her shoulder where the ghost stood, staring without expression as she talked to the policeman. "He can tell you a story that'll shock you to your core."

"You staying or going?"

Crystal was waiting out in the car to drop her home. "I'm going. Call if you need anything."

He'd already moved out of sight by the time she waved goodbye from the door. As she sat in the passenger side door, Crystal hooked up one eyebrow. "Has your ghost friend gone now? I didn't see any light."

"No. He's here." As Emily put her seatbelt on, she wondered if he'd ever leave. "He's still right here."

ON THE FOLLOWING TUESDAY, Crystal once again gave Emily a lift, this time to the graveyard. The police had made the decision to inter the bodies, and it didn't make sense to wait since nobody from their surviving family had known them in person. At best, they were snapshots in an old photo album, names on a family tree.

To Emily's surprise, Mrs Pettigrew had announced her intention to attend, and less surprising, Fred also came along for the ride.

"The children's section?" Cynthia exclaimed as they veered off the main path to join the few mourners gathering. "I mean, I suppose that's technically correct, but it's going to be weird since their friends are in their seventies."

Weird or not, Emily found it oddly soothing to stand amongst the bright colours and whirring toys of mourning found there. A plastic windmill's sales whirled so fast in the mild breeze it looked like a solid circle.

As the priest performing the ceremony recited the chosen passages, a hand crept into Emily's. She turned into the sad smile of Gladys, the nurse in attendance standing further back, a disgruntled look on her face.

"It's good they're getting a send-off," the elderly woman

said, waving across the grave at Fred, who stood in the shadow of a weeping willow tree.

"You can see him?" Emily asked, both comforted and frightened.

"He's been hanging around for days, now," Gladys said. "I can't work out what he wants."

"You and me both."

The caskets sat atop mechanical platforms. A groundsman stood back from the gathering, a respectful distance away, and pressed a button when the priest finished the eulogy. Each one lowered in turn, the engine groaning.

"Would anybody here like to say some words?"

Gladys disengaged her hand from Emily's and stepped forward. "I knew Billy, Tim, and Aaron well, once upon a time. They weren't my best friends. Partly because they were boys and partly because we were in a place that didn't encourage friendships. Still, we spent a lot of hours together and I wished them well. I'm glad they finally get the chance to rest in peace."

She bowed her head, then stepped back after a few minutes. The lucid twinkle in her eye startled Emily, used to seeing the woman in quite a different state.

"Oh, look." Gladys pointed. "They're here."

Emily followed the woman's gesture and saw the three ghosts pop their heads around the corner of the willow tree. A cheeky grin was plastered across their faces, and the leader turned to the others, a finger pressed up to his lips.

"Come on down, boys," Gladys shouted. "It's about time you gave up your hold on this place."

The priest cast a worried glance in her direction and the nurse stepped forward, placing a restraining hand on her arm.

Emily turned to her, "It's okay. I'm looking out for her."

The nurse tilted her head back to stare down the length of her nose. She gave a sniff as she stepped back, so reminiscent of Cynthia that Emily almost burst into laughter. Luckily, her sense of occasion remained intact, and she swallowed her mirth before returning her attention to the ceremony.

One by one, the ghost boys climbed into their graves, filled now with a steady glow of light. Crystal caught Emily's eye and jerked her chin at the light show, her smile beaming in recognition.

One ghost left.

Emily stared at Mr Wilmott, giving him a smile of encouragement. He returned the smile at first, then his face blanked into its usual sullen stare.

"Do you know what Freddie wants?" she whispered to Gladys.

When the lady turned to her, confusion blurred her features. Her previous alert gaze had clouded over. "What's that?"

Emily shook her head, trying to be grateful the boys had been able to move on. Sergeant Winchester stepped forward to drop a sod of earth into each grave, his lips calling out a prayer only the dead were privy to. She noticed another officer, dressed in his full regalia with three silver pips decorating the shoulders. The dreaded inspector from Christchurch.

When it was Emily's turn, she picked up a handful and shook a tiny amount of earth on top of each casket. The beautiful glow was diminishing with each second, leaving behind only the sad remains.

"Rest in peace," she whispered. "I hope you have more

fun playing in the next realm than you ever had the chance to do here."

By the time she stepped back into position, Gladys had moved on—the nurse strong-arming her back to the waiting car.

"I really thought I'd feel more of a sense of closure," Emily said to Agnes later. She'd dropped by the home to check up on her and Maude, scolding herself mightily that she was using their brief friendship as a pretext. The person she really wanted to speak to again was Gladys.

"Considering you didn't know the boys at all, I'm surprised you felt much of anything." Maybe sensing Emily's ulterior motive, the elderly lady appeared in quite a mood. "And I've still got this monstrous hole outside my window. It's all very well taking the bones out and away, but this serves as a reminder of what was down there."

The tents above the excavations flapped in the wind, a constant call drawing attention. "They shouldn't be like that for too long," Emily said, jerking back from the window as the Inspector strode into view.

"Great," Agnes muttered, pulling Maude into her lap. "More police. Just what we need."

The bulldog whined, trying to scramble free. It seemed she didn't appreciate her owner's mood any more than Emily did.

"If he's checking the scene out, it might mean they're about to fill the whole lot in," she suggested. "It might be a good sign."

"Or they've discovered yet another one. Since it appears it's central station for dead folks out there."

Although Agnes's face showed nothing but displeasure, the phrase caught Emily's funny bone. Despite her best efforts, she giggled.

"Fine. Laugh at me, why don't you? The shoe will be on the other foot one of these days and don't expect any sympathy from me when it is. I'd have swapped this horrible place out for a room in Christchurch, except the receivers have told us we're all staying put for the time being."

"They've already got the receivers in?" The surprise stopped Emily's laughter cold. "That was quick."

"Yeah, well. There's money to be made in us old folk, don't you know."

"I suppose they needed someone to hire staff with the main decision-makers under arrest."

"Shh." With a gleam of good humour in her eyes, Agnes held a finger to her lips. "Don't say it too loudly. We don't want everyone to find out."

"It's odd." Emily checked out the window just in time to see the inspector walking away. "This place used to operate as a reform school of sorts, and it seems the people running it belonged firmly in that camp."

"A breeding ground for criminals!" Agnes seemed delighted by the idea. "You know, when I was a kid, I always wondered what it would be like to rob a bank. Perhaps now's the time to find out."

"All the romance from the old bank robberies is gone these days." Emily winked. "You'd need to get a truck to do a smash and grab on an ATM."

"Or get hold of a computer to do a bit of credit card hacking."

They smiled at each other for a second, then burst out

laughing. It felt good to be back on an even keel. Even Maude joined in, snuffling and shaking her butt.

"I'm scared what will happen to my money if this place goes under," Agnes admitted. "Most of the profits from the sale of my house went straight into this unit."

"At a guess, they'll have that money set aside in a trust," Emily said, calling upon her old training. "Since most of it will be earmarked to go back to you or your estate after you pass on or sell, it'll be safe. It's the penalties and monthly fees where they make most of their profit."

"Well, that settles my mind some. If I became destitute at my age, I don't know what I'd do."

"You and Maude can always move in with me," Emily said, cupping the dog's face in her hand and blowing her a kiss. "There's enough room."

As long as you don't mind knocking about with some annoying ghosts.

"We do have standards, you know," Agnes said, looking down her nose. She managed to hold the expression for a second, then dissolved into giggles again. "How was the funeral?"

"Not too bad." Emily ran a hand through her hair and bounced on the edge of Agnes's bed. "It'd be a lot sadder if anyone actually knew them as children, but there was only Gladys and Maui in that position, and they seemed more relieved their friends were getting a decent burial at last."

"Much better than under the patio," Agnes agreed. "I pity the residents here who barbequed over top of them. It'd be enough to give me nightmares for the rest of my life."

Emily nodded and stood up. "I've got to go in a minute, but I promised Gladys I'd see her before I went off."

"Is your friend coming back for you?"

"No. Crystal had some appointments this afternoon, so I'm on my tod. I've got work piling up in the shop, though."

Agnes laughed and poked Emily in the ribs. "I meant because you don't have a car here. I'm not interested in the details of your day."

"Oh, thanks. That's lovely." Emily pouted for a second, then grinned. "I'll just catch an Uber."

"You mean, Frank."

Emily raised her eyebrows, not understanding.

Agnes sniggered. "You've got too used to the big city. There's not the same selection on offer in Pinetar, you know. If you call an Uber, you get Frank. If he's not on duty, you get no one."

"Good to know."

"It's even better to know that if you phone him direct on this number"—Agnes pulled a business card out of the stack on her desk—"he'll give you a discount."

Emily handed her phone over. "If you can pop that into my contacts, I'll let you keep the card."

She smiled as she walked through the winding tangle of corridors to reach the common room near Gladys's unit. She remembered just a week before when it seemed she'd never get a map of the place set in her mind. Now, she didn't think twice about it. Perhaps her mental capacity hadn't deteriorated as much as she'd feared.

"Do you have time to talk?" she asked Gladys when she found her resting against the frame of her favourite window.

Gladys offered an accommodating smile but the glaze in her eyes told Emily she had a struggle ahead of her. This was more than the confusion she'd seen clouding the woman's face before—it was drug-induced.

"Why's Fred here?" Gladys demanded. "What stopped him going home?"

She reached out for the ghost, her hand disappearing into his insubstantial flesh. When she tried for a second time, her fingers plunged into his chest.

"Where'd you go?" The elderly woman panted, distress contorting her face. "I can see you, why can't I touch?"

Emily caught Gladys's hand before she could reach out again. "How long have you been watching Fred?"

"Since they—" The lady turned and waved at the evidence tents. "When the plumber took an axe to the pipes, he popped up."

"An axe?" Emily frowned. "Why would the plumber do that?"

"Not the plumber, then." Gladys swayed on her feet, grabbing hold of the window frame to steady herself. "The other one. He wanted to chop down the tree."

"You mean the headmaster? Samuel Leuf?"

"No, the *other* other one." Gladys leaned into the window, pressing every inch of her body against the glass. Her mouth formed a seal, puffing her cheeks out. "Blow-fish," she announced happily, pulling back.

"Who was the other person with an axe, Gladys?" When the woman didn't respond, Emily tried a different tack. "Do you know who killed Fred?"

"The man with the axe." Gladys turned a deep frown toward her, stamping her foot. "I told you. He tried to chop down the tree."

Emily felt the conversation sailing away from her. She tried one last time to grab it back. "Who had the axe? Apart from the headmaster, who else chopped the tree?"

"The gardener, of course. It's his job, isn't it? He was meant to fell the oak to make room for the patio, and he chopped down Freddie instead."

CHAPTER EIGHTEEN

Even with the head nurse sitting with Gladys, and an ample rest period, the woman wouldn't share her story again. She sat, lower lip protruding like a sulking toddler. After the sergeant spent an hour using his powers of persuasion, he gave up the effort and quizzed Emily again.

"I'm sure of what she said. What she meant by it is less clear." Emily had already recited the conversation verbatim and found the repetition from the sergeant a tad insulting.

"We're just trying to ensure we don't waste time chasing up a false lead," Winchester said. The detective inspector from Christchurch stood outside, every glance at his watch winding the sergeant one notch further along the chain.

"Sure," Emily agreed. "I wouldn't want you to spent time with a potential eyewitness when you could be following up with—" She broke off and placed a finger on her cheek. "Remind me about those other leads?"

The sergeant's stern gaze warned her she might have gone one step too far. Emily didn't really care. The day had wrung out her emotions and the sooner it was over with, the better.

"Fine. But with this gibberish, I'm not even sure what the lead is meant to be."

"Eli Jamieson is the lead. The gardener."

"Who chopped up Frederick Wilmott with an axe?"

At his deadpan summary, Emily cast a worried look at Fred's ghost. He stood, staring out Gladys's window, impervious to the conversation going on just behind him.

"There'll be records, won't there?" she asked, suddenly thinking through the standard terms of employment for a retirement facility. "Most of these homes don't have a gardener on salary. They set up work orders for everything that needs to be done."

The sergeant tipped his head to one side, eyebrows raised in acknowledgement, and Emily felt a small thrill run through her. That would be the closest she got to recognition, so she took the gesture to heart.

"We'll need to get access to the old records," the sergeant said. "If they're locked on the computer, that'll take until we break the password."

Emily frowned. "Can't you just ask Margaret or Allain?"

"Oh!" The sergeant smacked a hand to his forehead in mock surprise. "Why didn't we think of that?"

"All right. There's no need to make fun of me. Have you asked the night porter, Erik?"

"That man has the memory of a goldfish."

Emily crossed her arms, tiredness making her angrier than the situation warranted. She remembered Erik having to call through to Margaret back when the ghost first uttered his own name. A pity he didn't have the call on a loudspeaker.

Suddenly, she snapped her fingers. "He wrote it down."

"What's that?"

"On the night he phoned up the receptionist for the password." Emily hooked her hand through the sergeant's elbow, dragging him to the front of the home. "He scribbled something on the blotter while he was talking to her. Or doodled," she added as another possibility struck her.

The current temp they'd hauled in to work the front desk seemed relieved to have something to do, even if it was just stand off to one side. "What're you looking for?" he asked. "I might be able to help."

"Is this the desk pad that was here when you started?" The sergeant tapped a finger on the completely clean sheet.

With a worried expression, the temp nodded. "I haven't changed around anything. All I did was tear off the top sheet."

While Emily's heart sank, Sergeant Winchester hooked the rubbish tin out from under the desk with a cry of triumph. He picked the large, screwed-up piece of paper from the trash and spread it out on the desk. "Bingo!"

"Shh!" Emily gave him a stern look. "Say things like that around here and you might cause a stampede."

The sergeant stared at her, dumbfounded, for a second, then snorted with laughter. "Do you mind if I sit here for a minute?" he asked the hovering temp, who shook his head.

"Go right ahead, mate. My whare is your whare and all that."

Armed with the password, it wasn't long before the printer sprang into life. "You were right," Sergeant Winchester said, inclining his head towards Emily. "One work order for the felling of two oak trees and the laying of a barbeque patio."

"Amended?"

He turned back to the computer. "Yeah. There's another printout on the file, for a quote from a bigger tree-felling company. Never acted on." The sergeant gave a low whistle. "Three-man job and at that price, I'd learn to love my old oak tree, too."

"He gave it a go, though." Emily pointed to the offending tree, now steeped in more innocent blood. "I noticed two sets of marks on the trunk. One old and healed, one much more recent." She clasped her hands together. "Is it enough?"

"It's nothing but should be good enough for a chat. Informal at this stage if you want to tag along. Just remember…"

He held up a finger and Emily finished the sentence for him, "Don't say anything unless you say so."

For all the rule made her feel like a child, it was with a lighter heart that she followed along behind the sergeant. He knocked on the door to the outside shed and Emily held her breath as they waited for a response.

From across the field, the inspector waved to them, deep in conversation with one of the new nurses on duty. The sergeant waved back, not giving any outward sign that he might have an interest in what they were about to do.

Just as Winchester raised his hand to knock again, the door pulled open. A man with unruly hair and bloodshot eyes stared out, yawning widely. "Yeah, what'd you want?"

"Eli Jamison?"

The man nodded, scratching the back of his neck. "That's me." He yawned again. "Sorry, you woke me up from my afternoon nap."

"Do you live here?"

Emily stood on tiptoe to gaze over the sergeant's shoulder. The old potting shed held a multitude of tools, seeds, and chemicals, along with a recliner chair complete with a pillow and a throw.

"No." Eli took a step out of the shed, pulling the door to behind him. "That'd be against the rules. I have the chair set up so I can nap when I need to. Sometimes I don't get a lot of sleep at home." When the sergeant didn't respond, he tilted up his chin and crossed his arms. "The boss doesn't mind."

"I'm sure he doesn't. He also doesn't mind us asking you a few questions about the patio over there."

The sergeant pointed, as though there might be some doubt what he was talking about. The broken-up slabs of concrete wouldn't have illuminated someone who didn't know already what the area had once been.

"What about it? If he wants to put it back to rights, it'll cost him the same as the first time. S'not my fault a pipe burst under it."

The sergeant frowned and leaned in closer. "You do realise a body was discovered underneath the barbeque area. Several bodies, in fact."

"Yeah." Eli tugged at his earlobe. "But they were old, weren't they? Nothing to do with me."

"Only a few of them were old. One of them was far more recent. Do you mind explaining the work you had to do originally to get this concrete laid?"

"Was there a dead body lying in the way, do you mean?" Eli laughed at his own joke. "I might be getting on a bit, but I reckon I'd have noticed." He nodded toward the side of the building. "There used to be an oak tree growing right up against the wall of that building. I chopped that down, then cut out the shape for the patio. I levelled it out nicely and used wood around the outside to keep it nice and tidy."

Eli's back straightened as he explained the workmanship, his chest puffing out. "It was a right sod to get most of it right. The dirt over there is mostly clay. I had to take a pick to most of it." He held out his hands, the palms a shade darker than the surrounding skin. "That's from the blisters. Didn't matter how many pairs of gloves I had on, they just kept bubbling up."

"Do you remember where the residents were during this time?"

Eli screwed his face up, shaking his head. "Nuh. Not my job to keep tabs on them." He went very still, folding his arms even tighter. "Why? You think one of them wandered off?"

"No." Sergeant Winchester gave a smile that showed off his eye-teeth. "I don't think that at all."

For long minutes, Eli held the sergeant's gaze, then he turned to one side and wiped his nose with the back of his hand. "Whatever. I don't keep tabs on them unless they walk into my field of work. If they do that, I chase them back out again."

"Were you using an axe to cut the tree down?" Emily asked, stepping back to avoid the heat from the sergeant's glare. "The one up by the house."

"Yeah, to start with. I used a saw as well. Why? You want to see?"

As the sergeant said no, Emily agreed and pushed forward, forcing Eli to step back and open the door wide again. "Is that the one?" she asked, pointing to the tool hanging on the wall.

"Yup." Eli pulled at his earlobe again, his eyes flicking to the sergeant as though to ask for permission before answering more fully, "That's it."

She moved closer, seeing some white sticker residue

halfway up the handle. Not the sort of thing that would last for long, even with casual usage. The dust would adhere and turn it grey or brown.

"It looks new."

"I keep my tools in good nick." Eli shouldered his way past her and pulled the axe down from the wall. He turned it back and forth, letting the sun catch it and shine off the thick blade. After hefting it once, twice, he put it back in its place. The outline made in black marker didn't quite fit.

"We could get this tested at the lab," Emily said, watching Eli break into a smile out of the corner of her eye. "They'd be able to tell for sure what it's been used for."

"Go right ahead, lady. I don't have any jobs that need it coming up, so it's no skin off my nose."

Emily reached out, then let her hand fall back to her side. "Or we could just let the lab test the marks in that old tree." She jerked her head at the oak, centre framed in the window.

"Eh?" Eli took a step back, his eyebrows coming together as his frown deepened.

"They can take the samples they have from the bones and match it to the axe marks in the oak tree." She examined Eli closely. "It's like matching bullets to guns, every axe has a unique signature. Why, if they can get a hit on those two samples, it doesn't matter what you have hanging on your wall."

The gardener took a step back, his arms flying up in defence when his foot landed on the sergeant's. "Careful," Winchester said in a deep growl. "You don't want to do anything right now that could be labelled as assault."

"The lab should also swab this area," Emily continued. "That's the great thing about DNA. It gets in everywhere and once it does, it's almost impossible to get out." She smiled at Eli, letting it broaden until her teeth showed. "The lab can get samples off metal or glass"—she swept her hand across the old, stained floorboards—"let alone something as porous as wood."

Once again, the gardener stepped back. This time, when he bumped up against the sergeant, he turned and pushed against him, gaining a moment of freedom to lunge out the door.

As the sergeant gave chase, yelling out behind him, Emily shuffled out of the dank shed to stand in the vibrant daylight. She had no idea what forensics could do with old axe marks—at a guess, probably nothing. But old bloodstains? Taken from the only logical place a man could hide a body he killed during the day?

The inspector cut Eli off before he could sprint halfway across the lawn. A second later, Sergeant Winchester tackled him from behind.

Emily blocked the sun with her hand as she stared at the play acting out. When she turned to see if the ghost Freddie had any reaction, he was gone.

CHAPTER NINETEEN

*I*t was a joy for Emily to walk into the charity shop later that afternoon, stuffed full of interesting tales to tell.

Gregory had been hard at work, filling in for her, so she only had to scan the items of interest to pick out the selections that would be suitable for auction. While she did so, she filled him in on all the latest happenings. Since he'd already experienced a ghost first-hand, she didn't need to hide any part of her story.

Pete received an expurgated version, focused more on the events in the shed than the resultant effect.

"Weren't you scared he'd attack you?" he demanded as Emily wound up her story. "If I was standing next to a killer with a wall full of tools at the ready, I think I'd just run away to be safe."

"I didn't really think of that," Emily admitted, ducking her head. "I suppose with the sergeant standing right there, it didn't seem a likely scenario."

"Maybe next time, it should. My troubled youth might be behind me, but I remember well enough that a police presence sometimes amplifies trouble rather than calming it."

"How was the funeral?" Gregory sat down near the counter, his cheeks flushed from the activity of the day. "Did the boys get a good send-off?"

"Good enough in the circumstances. It was weird not to have anyone except the priest and Gladys speaking. Even the few others who'd known them didn't step up—so many years had passed."

"I certainly hope my remains are found in a timely manner if I go too early." Gregory reached out and tapped his knuckles on the counter. "Touch wood."

"How about you just stay out of trouble and avoid the situation altogether?" Pete narrowed his eyes at the young man and Emily frowned.

"Is there something I should know that you're not telling me?"

"There've been a few suspicious types hanging around after work," Pete said, pointing a finger at Gregory. "And they're not out there to sell to me."

"They're not selling and I'm not buying." The young man's face flushed, a slow creep of colour moving at the same languorous pace as everything else he did. "When I asked around town to see if there was any other volunteer work, the police asked me to be a big brother type figure for them."

"Is that true?" Pete frowned, his face still registering suspicion. "They looked the same age as you."

Gregory scowled. "They're only fifteen. How old do you think I am?" He shifted on his seat. "It's really hard to find activities to do with them. Everything is either geared towards younger kids or older adults."

"How are you at skating?"

Now it was Gregory's turn to narrow his eyes. "On a board?"

"No. On roller skates. There's a derby set up down at Pinetar Beach at the old hall. We've got a few teams together. You'll be welcome to join if you can keep up."

Emily laughed in surprise. "We've got a roller derby?"

"We do and since the average age of the competitors is mid-thirties, everyone is far too careful right now." Pete flashed his gap-toothed smile. "It might be fun to inject some young blood into the event. A lack of fear is a great advantage."

"I'd love to come down." When Pete laughed, Emily punched him on the arm. "I meant as a spectator, not a competitor. You allow those, don't you?"

When she left the shop for the day, Gregory had a new sport to practice and she had a front row seat at the derby for the following week.

The smile on Emily's face fell away as soon as she walked through the front door at home. Cynthia stood in the kitchen with her arms folded and her lower lip poking out. Beside her, arms and mouth hanging loosely, was Fred Wilmott's ghost.

"I don't see why you're so upset," Cynthia said as Emily burst into tears of despair. "You're not the one who has to keep him occupied all day long."

"I really thought he'd moved on this time," Emily managed between sobs. "There's nothing more I can think to do. We've found his killer, we've laid his friends to rest. If those didn't help him move on, what's left?"

"Have you tried asking him?"

A spurt of rage rose up in Emily. "Of course, I've tried. He never answers. Do you?" She spun around to stare at the ghost, head-on. "You never say anything."

"He told you his name," Cynthia pointed out. "And he spelled out Astrid on the keyboard. I don't suppose you have something else he could use to communicate?"

"Fred can talk if he wants to," Emily said, folding her arms to contain the volcano bubbling in her chest. "There's no impediment. Maui told us he just stopped talking after the incident with the boys."

Cynthia shot a quick glance at Mr Wilmott, then leaned forward to whisper, "You mean the death of three of his best friends? If that kind of thing ever happened to me, I'd probably shut up for a while, too."

"That would be a blessing," Emily spat out. She knew she was being moody and horrible but for the moment, didn't care. "And when have you ever had three friends?"

"Maybe he won't tell you what he needs to move on because you're such a grouch." Cynthia raised her eyebrow, taking the verbal blows in her stride. "Did you ever think of that?"

"I've thought of everything. It hasn't helped."

"You don't even talk directly to Fred, have you noticed that? Even now, when you're desperate to find out how to move him along, you're only talking about him to me. The only times you address him directly are to tell him off." Cynthia moved over to stand beside Mr Wilmott, an act of solidarity. "Why don't I leave you two alone to discuss things?"

"Because he can't talk and I can't read," Emily said with a sigh. "And you're right." The words—*as usual*—sounded in her head. "I'm sorry, Fred. Can you tell us something to lead us onto the right track? I've tried everything I can think of and I'm out of answers."

The ghost stared blankly at her, then switched his gaze to the floor.

Emily groaned and ran her hands through her head. "I just don't know what to do."

"Do you still have that weird typewriter hanging about?" Cynthia waved at the table where it had been sitting. "We could see if Fred wants to use that again."

"It's been auctioned." Emily hid her face behind her hands, shutting everything out as she tried to come up with an idea—any idea. "Just a moment."

She sprang to her feet and hurried into the bedroom. In the wardrobe, she felt along the top shelf above the clothes hangers, pulling out a large box. Inside were a selection of board games.

They hadn't been played in decades—even when they were children, Emily and Harvey hadn't been big on so-called 'fun for all the family.' Still, the games were something her parents had treasured, so when they died, she couldn't bring herself to toss them away.

"Here we are!" she cried out, holding aloft the Scrabble set in its original dark green box.

"I hate to break it to you, Scarface, but we're going to whip you at that game. You wouldn't even be able to tell if we're cheating."

"Not for playing the game. For the tiles." Emily moved into the lounge and spread out the letters. "How about it, Mr Wilmott? Do you feel up to telling us anything more?"

Peanut ran into the room, nosing at the wooden pieces and trying to bat them away. Emily lifted him up and held the cat on her lap, stroking him as she waited to see if Fred would play.

It took a good half hour before he shuffled over, then another ten minutes of staring before he picked letters out.

"Astrid again." Cynthia sounded disappointed as she reported the latest word. She folded her arms and shook her head. "Could you give us something new? We already know you've got a girlfriend."

Another hour passed before he pointed out letters again. Emily had to call Cynthia in from the back yard where she'd gone to watch the sunset. Or to mope.

"Gang. Now that sounds more promising." She gave Fred a poke in the ribs. "Tell us more about your troubled youth."

"Don't tease him," Emily scolded. "Otherwise, we might be here all night."

Cynthia snorted. "Like either of us has anything better to do."

Still, she settled back, watching as the ghost picked out letters with all the speed of a glacier moving down a hillside. "Wolf," she said at last. "Gangs and wolves. Now, that does sound like an interesting tale."

"We don't have wolves in New Zealand," Emily said idly, listening to the satisfied purr from Peanut. "Unless we've got some werewolves stored away somewhere, I don't know about."

"He's just picking out the same letters," Cynthia said with a sigh as Mr Wilmott kept pointing. "Gang. Wolf."

"Do you mean Wolfgang?" Emily asked. "Like a name?"

The ghost didn't reply. His only response was to point out the same sequence of letters again.

"Astrid and Wolfgang." Cynthia sat back and stretched out her legs. "Sounds like he might have something against the Germans."

"Or something for them, considering one was his girlfriend." Emily knelt to pick up the tiles from the carpet, not wanting to leave them out to stand on by accident. They might not have the pure fire-power of Lego but she bet they'd hurt just the same.

"I guess we'll start looking into them with more care tomorrow," Emily said after catching Fred's eye. "Astrid Wallheimer, right?"

It might have been her imagination but for a second, the ghost appeared to smile.

CHAPTER TWENTY

"It's a pity they didn't have a bigger digital footprint back then." Gregory stretched out his back, his hands waving high above his head. "If they'd only thought to come up with Facebook in the sixties, it'd make this research a doddle."

"Bit hard to invent social media before you had the computers to run it on," Emily pointed out. "And I'm pretty sure even the most enthusiastic time-traveller wouldn't be interested in changing that many things just to help us out with our one query."

"Yeah. I've been uniformly disappointed with time travellers," the young man muttered, turning back to the job. "So lazy. So unwilling to meddle."

"Be nice if everyone could just concentrate on what they're meant to be doing," Cynthia chimed in. "We might get this sorted out before the end of the century if everyone stays on task."

As if the laptop heard her, Gregory gave a hoot of triumph and turned the screen around for Emily to see. "That's her, right?"

"I think so," she said, squinting her eyes to make the image less blurry. "That looks like it's from the same series of photos that Michael and Maui have."

"It says here, it's from a biography written by Sheila Wainscoting, about her time working as a matron in various boarding schools."

"Matron?" Emily pushed the computer back to Gregory. "Maui mentioned her a few times. Is she still alive?"

"No."

Emily frowned. "Did you look?"

"She'd be well into her hundreds by now. I think we can take it as read that she's long gone."

"What about the book?"

Gregory tapped at the keys, scanning the information on the screen at lightning speed. A strange contrast to his physical movements.

"It's available as a PDF on the website. Hopefully, it's scanned as words rather than just images, then we can search—Ha! Got it."

He swivelled the screen around towards her, then caught himself. "It's got a bit in here about her time at Oakhaven and mentions Astrid three times in the text."

"Anything we can follow up on?"

The young man dove into the task, biting on his lower lip as he scrolled through the pages. "Here's another photograph from when she worked in a dairy. Apparently, it was Sheila—Matron—who found her the job."

Emily scooted around to peer over his shoulder. "It's fascinating, looking up these old histories."

"Not much older than you."

She stared at the back of Gregory's neck, thinking of all

the horrible ways she could enact revenge. "Twenty years is quite a difference. Even at my age."

"I suppose."

"What about the family who employed her?" Emily paused. "I presume it was a family business."

"The parents are dead, but it looks like the son is still alive." He pulled up the photograph again, pointing to the boy who looked about ten. "Did you want me to get his details?"

"Yes, please." The thought of talking to another complete stranger twisted Emily's stomach, but she hoped Crystal might be talked into coming along for the ride. "Is there anything else in the book?"

"Not much to help you out. It says she left to pursue her religious vocation. Do you think that means she became a nun or something?"

Emily pulled her mouth down. "It could, I suppose. Unless it's a code word for something else. Maui also said the school liked to play up how much it was helping the children forced to attend. Perhaps the matron was doing a bit of that, too."

Gregory sat back on his heels, typing the few details he'd learned into Emily's phone. "If Astrid was Mr Wilmott's girlfriend, he'd probably be miffed to learn she went into a nunnery."

The phrase struck Emily's funny bone and when she stopped laughing, she glanced over to the corner where the ghost sat. "He doesn't look impressed, one way or the other. Apparently, when the boys died at the school, they were trying to distract the headmaster so Fred could sneak out to meet her."

"I'm not sure if that sounds romantic or like a stalker."

"There was no suggestion by Maui it was anything

other than a reciprocal relationship. Besides, he never got to meet up with her in the end."

"Do you think she was sitting at a train station or something, waiting for a lover who never arrived?"

Emily stared into the middle distance as her mind conjured up a heart-breaking image. "I hope not." She gave Gregory an elbow in the ribs. "I think I prefer your stalker theory over that one."

She played back the address he'd loaded into her phone. "That's just around the corner. I could go there straight after work."

"You could go there now. I'll take this lot down to the auction house for set-up. It'll be a nice change to get out of this heat-trap."

The attic above the charity shop became stuffy by the afternoon. Emily was looking forward to the winter when she'd freeze to death instead.

"If you're sure you'll be okay. I don't mind coming with you and introducing you to everyone."

Gregory rolled his eyes. "Unless there's a rabid dog on the loose there, I think I'll handle the place okay." He clapped her on the shoulder when Emily continued to frown. "Come on, Grandma. I'm a grown man."

"You won't get much older if you call me that." Emily smiled and pinched his cheek. "Such a good boy!"

The poky flat at the back of eighty-four Severson Drive made Agnes Myrtle's room at Stoneybrook appear grandiose in comparison. The front door was a ranch slider, with the curtain only pulled halfway. It let Emily see into the three-metre by four-metre house in all its glory.

"I'm not buying nothing," the man who answered the door said before she could get a word in. "Don't care what it is, I don't want it and I don't need it."

"David Llewellyn?"

The man's eyes narrowed, and he thrust his face closer to Emily's, scanning her up and down before retreating. "Who wants to know?"

"My name's Emily Curtis and I'm trying to find information about someone you may have known when you were younger. Astrid Wallheimer?"

Although David's face didn't alter its expression, she judged his lack of surprise to be a good thing.

"You a relative of hers?"

"No." Emily was about to add more information, then she clamped her lips together. She didn't want to play out her entire hand before he'd even looked at his cards.

As the silence lengthened, she glanced over the man's shoulder. A photograph on the wall showed the same dairy as the one Gregory had sourced earlier. No matter what else, it meant she was on the right track, at least.

"She worked for my parents for a while. A long time ago."

Emily nodded, once again having to stem a tide of words from flooding forth.

Another short silence. A minute passed. Two.

"You better come in," David said, standing back from the door and giving a sigh of effort. "I don't need you standing out there getting the neighbour's tongues wagging."

"Thank you."

He moved aside a large collection of old magazines, dumping them on the floor instead. From habit, Emily noted the pictures and judged the age. They were all for model enthusiasts with the colour schemes dating them back to the eighties and nineties.

Along the walls were shelves showcasing various models. Stacked at one end were boxes, still factory sealed. Emily's fingers itched to inspect them, but she forced her attention back to David. She was here to find out about Astrid, not price model kits for a potential auction.

"Don't know if I'll be much help. Astrid only worked for Mum and Dad for six months. The clearest thing I remember is her leaving without giving much notice. Mum couldn't come to my sports day because of it."

"Sorry to hear that. I'm trying to track Astrid down and the more I can find out about her, the better. Do you know why she left in a hurry?"

He shrugged. "Nobody told me anything in those days." David tilted his head to one side. "Not just me. Every kid was on a need-to-know basis and there wasn't a lot any parent deemed as need-to-know."

Emily nodded. She remembered that from her own childhood. These days, parents treated children as fully-fledged members of the household for the most part. When she was growing up, it was a case of being seen and not heard. Kids weren't just shorter than adults, they operated on a completely different level.

"What was she like?"

"Pretty cheerful, though she didn't have a lot to be happy about. Compared to the girl my parents had in before her, she seemed grateful to have the job. The one before—Susan, I think her name was—acted like my mum should kiss the ground she walked on just for deigning to turn up on time."

Although he issued the statement without any sense of humour, Emily laughed politely, hoping to ease the

179

atmosphere. She was getting a sense of entitlement, all right, but it wasn't from any shop girl.

"Do you know where she was living?"

At that, David's face screwed up with glee. "She was one of them naughty girls. Came from Oakhaven and was saving up money to get a flat because her parents didn't want her back. There were lots of kids around town like that. Dad sometimes made me check their pockets before we let them leave the store because half of them were thieves."

Emily thought back to Maui's assertion. *They'd never believe me.* The sadness dragged at her, not helped by the expression of gloom spread across the ghost's face.

"What else do you remember about her? Was she pretty?"

"No," he scoffed. "Not that I was at an age when I was looking for that, anyway. But she was about as attractive as a dump truck and twice as fat." He pulled at his nostrils for a second, then jerked out a handkerchief to catch a large sneeze. "I hope that's from the pollen," he grumbled. "I can't be dealing with a cold. Not at my age."

Emily cast about in her mind for another question but couldn't think of anything more to ask. It was all too long ago. Nobody would know more than this man. A goose chase, that's all it was. The ghost would stay on, glaring at her forever, until the day she died.

"Actually," David held up one finger, frowning, "I might know why she moved on, after all." He blew his nose again, staring in disgust at the mess before he folded the hanky and shoved it back in his pocket. "I remember hearing later, on the grapevine, that they'd expelled her."

"From Oakhaven?"

David scowled at her. "Of course, from Oakhaven.

That's what I've been telling you, isn't it?" He scratched at the receding hairline crawling up his temple. "Yeah. Come to think of it, I'm sure that was how it went down. She was so naughty the worst school in town expelled her." He grinned. "I guess you can cross university off the list of possible places she went afterwards."

An expulsion should be recorded somewhere. Of that, Emily felt sure.

Probably in a box of records at the department of 'no one's ever going to need these again,' her mind responded in a doleful tone.

As though reading her mind, David continued, "They used to print those in the local paper. It was like a warning to the businesses around town, so they didn't accidentally hire those kids for a job."

"The Pinetar Gazette?"

"Yeah. The one and only. Though, that's a joke now as it's run out of Christchurch, these days."

He stood up, grunting with the effort. Emily followed suit a moment later, grateful the interview was at an end. Outside, she took a deep breath of fresh air, holding it in her lungs for a second, like it would scrub her lungs clean.

"The library," she whispered under her breath. If any place in town was going to have back-copies dated in the sixties, it would be there.

CHAPTER TWENTY-ONE

As Emily entered the air-conditioned luxury of the library, she spotted the librarian with a queue of people ready to check their books out. Although the system was somewhat automated—compared to the manual ink stamps that had been the modus operandi when she was younger—it still took a few minutes for the backlog to clear.

In the meantime, she wandered over to the graphic novels arranged on a shelf at the head of an aisle. Until the librarian had suggested it on a previous visit, Emily had thought books were something lost to her. Between the vibrant pictures and the discovery of audiobooks, she'd been granted a new lease on bookworm life.

"How can I help?" the woman asked as she approached.

While Emily explained her mission, she realised she didn't know the woman's name.

"Georgia," the librarian replied with a stilted laugh when she asked. She tapped the nametag, then blushed, remembering Emily's disability.

"The old papers are on microfiche," she said. "We had a grant from the parent company when they moved the gazette out of town. It took a long time, but they're all on there now."

"The man I spoke to said school expulsions used to be listed."

Georgia nodded. "That sounds about right. They had them alongside the court convictions if I remember. Lumped together as though they were of equal concern."

She set the machine up with the correct year and scrolled through the pages. With only an approximate date to go on, based on Maui's recollections, Emily had expected the search to take a long time. Instead, on the second paper, Georgia gave a thumbs-up sign.

"Astrid Wallheimer. Expelled from Oakhaven School for behaviour unbecoming to a lady."

Emily snorted, waiting for the joke, then her eyes opened wide as she understood the librarian was serious. "That's the reason they gave?" She shook her head. "I don't even know what it means."

"It'll be a code for something, but I can only guess what. Maybe wearing trousers or spitting at a teacher." Georgia's lips pressed into a thin line. "I'm sure nothing that warranted an announcement in the paper."

"The man I spoke to said Astrid left his parent's employ without giving any notice. I wonder instead if the reverse was true. They saw this and fired her."

"Could be. Did you want to search for anything else?"

Emily shook her head. "No, thanks. You've been very helpful. I kind of hoped it would say where she went to next, but I can't imagine what article would feature that."

"In those days, I'd imagine she moved towns and tried again where nobody knew her name. Maybe up the road in Ashburton or down in Christchurch. Probably the latter since it's easier to get lost in a bigger city."

To get lost. Unfortunately, that's exactly what Astrid appeared to have done.

As Emily was leaving, she had a sudden thought. "I found a reference to her in an old book, it said she left school to pursue a religious vocation. Nothing about being expelled at all."

Georgia raised her eyebrows. "Another code?

"Possibly." Emily smiled forlornly. "I'm sorry. I don't have much to go on."

"It could mean exactly that. Oakhaven was a Catholic School before the government took it over. I'd imagine it still had ties in that community and a lot of the reform students were pushed towards the church."

"Really? Where would she have gone if that's the case?"

"Try St Anne's. They're the closest parish."

CRYSTAL WAS happy to accompany Emily on another road trip, even one on such late notice and short duration.

"I must say, all these adventures are keeping me young," she remarked as she pulled onto State Highway One. "These days, I never know where'll I'll end up when I start the day."

"Hopefully, back home safe in your bed in time for a good night's sleep." Emily's train of thought sparked an enormous yawn. "That's what I'm praying for."

When they pulled into the gravelled church carpark, Emily was awed by the stained-glass windows. "I think my Anglican upbringing cheated me," she said to Crystal. "We never had anything as spectacular to look at as that."

"It's what's on the inside that counts." Crystal didn't

glance twice at the ornate structure, striding straight to the door and knocking loudly.

"I think you can just walk in," Emily said as she joined her, pointing at the opening hours sign. "That sounds like an open invitation."

Crystal pushed open the heavy wooden door, shuddering as the hinges gave a horror-movie squeal. "When does the vampire crawl out of the coffin?"

"Not until midnight."

The church had tea light candles, some winking with fire, some unlit, on a shelf opposite the door. Photographs were arranged above them, along with a collection of personal odds and ends—jewellery, ornaments, small toys.

Pews stretched half the length of the room, ending in a pulpit at one end and a wide aisle at the other. That was the space Emily headed towards, figuring someone might be in an office behind.

"Hello?" she called out. "Is anybody home?"

"You sound like a door-to-door salesman," Crystal muttered. "At least put some oomph into it." A second later she bellowed, "My kingdom for a priest."

A head popped around the entrance, followed a second later by the tallest, thinnest body Emily thought she'd ever seen. If the rack were still in common use, she'd wonder what the man had done to deserve such a stretching.

"I think I might be the priest you're seeking," the man said with a smile. "How can I help you?"

"We're tracing the whereabouts of someone who might have come into your order back in the sixties. Astrid Wallheimer? She was originally at a school in Pinetar, but we think she came here next."

"You mean she came here as a novitiate?" When Emily nodded, even though she had no idea, he put a hand up to his chin. "There was an order of nuns attached to this parish back then, but they've since been absorbed into a church in Christchurch."

Emily nodded, keeping her smile fixed in place despite the sinking feeling in her stomach. "Which church would that be?"

"Hold on one moment." The priest held up a finger before walking out of the room. He returned a few minutes later, carrying a large leather-bound tome. "We keep all the records associated with this parish, even after the order based here disbanded. What year did you say?"

While Emily recited the information, he flipped through the pages, finally happening upon the correct entry. "Here we go." He beamed a smile at full wattage, and she thought for a moment it was a pity he'd gone into the priesthood. There were many a young woman in Pinetar who would have been glad to make his acquaintance.

Emily stood on the other side of Crystal, who peered over the priest's shoulder to see what he'd found. "This says she left the order after six months. That's not very long."

"No, not a long stay. She must've been a postulant, or an aspirant, then. They live within the community for a while to see if it's a good fit."

He shuffled through the pages, searching out further entries. "Ah, but hopefully this indicates she wasn't completely averse to our charms. It shows her in attendance at this parish for years afterwards. The last entry is dated nineteen seventy-two. Either she stopped attending mass, or she moved on."

"Would the church have any records of her if she did move away?" Emily bit her lip as she waited for the answer, a shake of the priest's head.

"But this says a different name," Crystal said, pointing

to an entry on the page. "This is Astrid Wall instead of Wallheimer. Does that mean she got married or something?"

"It could be a choice." The priest flipped back to the original entry. "It changed sometime between her arrival and her first attendance as a standard parishioner. Based on the similarities in the name, I'd assume she shortened her surname. I can't see a marriage record and it would be a striking coincidence."

"We've been looking for the wrong name," Emily said, putting her hands up to cool her flushed cheeks. "No wonder Gregory couldn't turn anything up on the computer."

"Well, then." The priest closed the book with a thump. "I'm glad I could help. Is there anything else you need?" He waggled his eyebrows at Crystal. "Someone's kingdom you want to dispose of?"

They left, still laughing from a mixture of the priest's humour and pure relief. "I hope this gets us closer," Emily said, waving to the ghost who'd remained sitting in the back seat of the car. "Although, it's nice to find any trail, even if it peters out."

"Try on Facebook," Crystal said when they got into the car. When Emily looked blank, she held out her fingers and clicked, "Give me your phone and I'll do it. Let's see what we can turn up under the new name."

Emily handed it across, feeling the pang when it left her fingertips. Even with the device in full view, separation anxiety struck. Ten years ago, her mobile phone had been a burden that she hoped never rang because it just meant more work. Now, it was a lifeline for navigating a world not designed for the illiterate.

"Here's some information," Crystal said after just a few

minutes. "There're a lot of photos on this page. The woman apparently didn't know the meaning of a privacy setting. Oh!"

She stared at the phone for a moment, her face still with shock, then she passed the device back.

"What is it?" Emily squinted, unable to decipher any meaning.

"I'm so sorry, it appears the trail petered out, after all."

"She stopped posting?"

"She stopped living." Crystal's voice thickened, and she cleared her throat. "Astrid Wall is dead."

EMILY INSISTED they travel to the gravesite. Crystal didn't want to and, in truth, neither did she, but with Mr Wilmott seated, unmoving, in the back seat she needed to at least try to get rid of him.

"Every time I try to do what I think you want, we end up in exactly the same place." Emily wrapped her arms so tightly across her chest, it hurt to breathe. "Why can't you just tell me? I can chase down these dead ends for a million years and never get it right."

The grave wasn't new. Astrid had passed away seven years before. If it had been the space of a few days or a few weeks, Emily might have held out more hope. But seven years?

It didn't surprise her too much when Mr Wilmott stayed firmly in tow.

"If your ghost friend can't talk, is there another way he can signal you?"

Emily kicked at a clump of sod on the ground. "We've

tried all that. If there is, he's done his best to keep the method hidden."

The two women stood beside each other, staring at the grave.

"Her obituary said she died in hospital," Crystal said after a long silence. "Maybe that's the key to it all. We could try visiting the ward where she died."

"Even if the hospital would tell us, I doubt it'd do any good." Emily tried her best to keep the tears back, but her nose ran, and her breathing grew heavy. "This is where her body lies. If this doesn't trigger any pool of light, I can't think the room she died in would be any better. A thousand patients must have lain in the same spot since."

"I guess you just need to wear a blindfold to bed."

Emily turned to her friend, puzzled. "I don't follow."

"Since he's going to be there, staring at you while you sleep every night, the best you can do is pretend not to see him."

The horror of the thought—nights stretching out into years—tugged Emily's breath away. It mixed up her head until she could do nothing to get rid of it but laugh.

"It's not funny," she insisted, gasping for breath between bouts. "I don't know why I'm laughing."

"Because some things are so dreadful you just have to give in." Crystal joined her, holding her sides as the fits carried on for too long.

Finally, they both straightened up, using each other for support.

"What's Mr Wilmott doing now?"

"Staring at the ground." Emily cocked her head to one side and leaned over, checking there was nothing to see. "It's what he does best."

"The poor thing." Crystal sighed and rubbed her hand up Emily's back. "And that goes double for you."

"I wish I had the chance to pity someone for a change," Emily said, groaning. "I felt so sure for a while there we were on the right track."

"What else has he told you, apart from his girlfriend's name?"

Emily opened her mouth to answer, then felt a tug in the back of her mind.

"What?" Crystal leaned forward, her expression worried. "What's going on?"

"There's something. A memory." Emily hissed out a breath. "I almost had it, but it slipped away."

"Something about Mr Wilmott or about Astrid?"

"I don't know." Emily stamped her foot into the ground, eyebrows knitting together. "It's gone."

"If it came once, it'll come again." Crystal bent over to touch her fingertip to the gravestone, then walked along the path back to the car. "I hope you don't mind if we stop at the next dairy for something to eat. I'm starving."

"Remember when they used to have five cent mixes?"

"You're showing your age. In my day, it was ten cents, or twenty."

"Fifty got you at least one gobstopper."

"My mother always said they made me lose weight because I sucked on them for so long, I skipped entire meals."

Emily stopped in her tracks, the threads in the back of her mind knitting together. "Maui said Astrid got fat after starting work in the dairy. He said she ate too many sweets while the store owner wasn't looking."

"A bit harsh, I'll grant you." Crystal patted the ample

expanse of her own stomach. "But there's nothing wrong with a bit of padding."

"The boy whose family she worked for said she was fat, too. When I looked at her photographs, I could see her being one to gain weight easily. She had that rounded look, already."

Crystal had stopped walking when Emily did and now stared at her with open concern. "Look, I know it's awful that women are judged on their appearance, but that's how things are. Back then, you can expect it'd be even worse."

Emily tugged on her friend's sleeve, trying to sort out the words to bring her dancing thoughts together. "She was expelled from the school. From *reform* school. You remember Maui said most of the girls there had been caught doing stuff like kissing boys behind the bike sheds?"

"Yeah, I remember. It got my back up."

"Mine, too. But maybe, in some cases, that's the only way those girls knew how to express affection." Emily stared at the ground, not wanting to check with Mr Wilmott in case she saw another dead-end in his eyes.

"The article in the paper wrote her expulsion was due to behaviour unbecoming to a lady. I just thought it was some old-fashioned tosh, but it means something. It meant something. Just like spending six months in a nunnery immediately afterwards meant something."

Crystal shrugged. "Meant what?"

"Astrid was pregnant. They expelled her from the school because she was about to have a baby."

"Steady on. I don't think they let you join a religious order when you're an unwed mother. Especially not back then."

"She didn't join them. They *housed* her. It's part of what a lot of these organisations did at the time. They took in the mothers and placed their babies out for adoption. Some places did it within a few weeks, but many nunneries allowed the mothers six months to change their minds."

Finally, unable to bear the thought of what she'd do now if she was wrong, Emily turned her gaze to Fred. The ghost smiled, tears running down his face.

"We're not searching for his old girlfriend. He wants to say goodbye to his son."

CHAPTER TWENTY-TWO

If the priest was surprised to see them for the second time in a day, he hid the emotion well.

"You're right. The order did cater for unmarried mothers but I'm afraid I'd never be able to let you see those records. They're sealed at the very least, if not destroyed." He held his hands out to either side, a stick insect mimicking remorse. "As much as I'd love to help you, I can't."

"What about the sisters who would've been working in the convent at the time?" Emily banged her hand on the pew in excitement. "Your employment records aren't sealed, are they?"

"You're talking about so long ago, it probably won't do you any good. I can give you a list, but if you're serious about tracking a baby down after so long, a private investigator might be a better bet."

"How d'you know we're not private investigators?" Crystal asked and Emily could practically see her friend composing the business card in her mind as she spoke.

The priest leaned forward, presumably to hide a blossoming grin. "If you are, please show me your ID." He looked up, an eyebrow cocked, then inclined his head towards them. "In that case, I think we've reached the end of the road, here."

"What would you give a PI that you won't give us?" Emily demanded as he escorted them to the door.

"A hard time," the priest said with a smile. "And a lesson on what information is and isn't publicly available, in stronger language than what I've given you."

The expulsion from the church might have been gentle, but it was also final.

"What now?" Crystal drummed her fingers on the steering wheel. "He's right. If those records are sealed, the only person who might be able to find anything out is the person we're searching for."

"There must be some way to do it." Emily turned and watched the emotions play out across Fred's face. The transformation from sullen to fully animated was incredible. She didn't want to watch the change in reverse.

"Wolfgang?" she asked, and Mr Wilmott nodded. "Try searching online for that name. There can't be many men around here called that, surely."

"If the adoptive parents even let him keep the name."

"Maybe she changed her mind?" When Crystal glanced up, brows raised, Emily explained, "If Astrid spent six months with the baby, perhaps she managed to work out a way to keep him."

"There wasn't any mention of him on her gravestone, so I'm going to say no to that one."

"They could've fallen out later."

Crystal cocked her right eyebrow at Emily until she fell silent. Yeah, it was a long shot.

"Okay. We have three results in Canterbury. One has a birthday at completely the wrong time of the year. One has everything in his profile set to private. The last looks like he's seventeen, tops."

Emily peered over at the phone, squinting to see if that improved the images. "Why can't they take a nice profile shot?" she grumbled. "Standing still and face to the camera."

"Because they're human beings posting on a social media site, not corporate robots lining up for an ID card. Oh, that's a good idea, though. I'll try the same names on Linked In."

After a short pause, Crystal shook her head, blowing her fringe out of her eyes. "Nada. I'll put in a friend request for the guy obsessed with privacy since the other two are no-gos."

"How long will that take?"

Crystal gave her a curious look, then tapped on the phone again. "How is this possible?" She stared openly at Emily until she shifted in her seat, feeling exposed. "How can you not have a profile on Facebook?"

"I liked Bebo. When everyone got off it, I couldn't be bothered trying again. It was just a distraction from life."

"Yeah." Crystal mugged at her. "That's the whole point!"

"I guess this conversation is a way to distract me from my question." Emily waved her finger in the air. "And I further guess, that means you don't know."

"Of course, I don't know how long it'll take for someone to friend me back. For all I know, he's already checked out my profile and decided that he'd rather walk along a road of embers to hell than accept a request from me."

Emily chuckled, then buried her face in her hands. "There must be some other way. We can't get this close to the answer, then lose it because someone chose the wrong setting online."

"You know, the whole private investigator idea might not be a bad one." Crystal tapped away at the phone again, leaving Emily wondering what her pay-as-you-go plan was about to debit to her account. "There're a few in Canterbury or Hurunui we could try."

"Any in Pinetar? I think I'd prefer to meet someone face to face."

"That doesn't sound like you."

"It'll make it easier to plead poverty if they can see the state I'm in." Emily ruffled up her hair into a crazy mass and undid her cardigan so she could re-button it wrong. "What'd you reckon?"

"There's pleading poverty and then there's not getting through the front door because you look like a bag lady. Tone it down a little and hook your hair back to showcase your scar."

Emily pulled the hair back, trying to tuck it in behind her ear—a hard ask for her short, grey curls. She struck a pose, chin up, lower lip pooching out. "What about now?"

"Oh, now you look irresistible."

Crystal put the phone down to clap and Emily snatched it up before her bill could be run any higher.

She flicked back to the social media profiles, scrutinising each profile image. The man with the wrong birthday seemed familiar. Like an old friend she vaguely remembered from school.

"This is exactly six months past the incident."

"What is?" Crystal leaned over, staring at the page upside-down. "Yeah. That's a pity because he's otherwise the right age."

"No!" Emily held up the screen, placing it next to the

ghost's face, then comparing each feature, one by one. "I mean, if Astrid stayed in the nunnery for six months, then her baby wouldn't have been adopted out until the end."

Crystal opened her eyes wide. "You think they changed the date?"

"It's the sort of thing that might've happened back then. A birthday's just a number, isn't it? It'd mean more for the new parents to record the day they adopted their son and brought him home than the actual date he was born."

"But the birth certificate would show the right day."

"Yeah. But it's not as though this is a government ID. You can put any date you like in here. If his parents celebrated the day, he became part of their family rather than his actual birth…"

Crystal finished off the thought. "Then he might've grown used to saying it. Does it have an address or something?"

Emily frowned at the phone. "No. But there's some way to geotag people on here, to locate them." She pulled her seatbelt on. "Let's go back and talk to Gregory. He's the right age to know about stuff like that."

"I think they turned off most of that information," Gregory said an hour later, checking the mobile. "People kicked up a stink over it."

"I'm not surprised," Crystal said, clutching her shawl closed over her chest. "The idea someone can do that freaks me right out."

"On the other hand…" Gregory held out the phone towards Emily, pointing at a picture on the screen. "Recognise this place?"

"It's the stone cottage outside Belfast."

"Yeah. And fix on that tree in the third house along. The camellia."

Emily nodded, waiting for him to get to the point.

"It's the same bush here, in the photograph of him and his wife. You can see it out the front window, through the net curtain."

She had to enlarge the photograph to see exactly what Gregory had caught, but once she saw it, the plant was unmistakable.

"How long ago was the photograph taken?"

"I don't know but it was only posted a few weeks ago."

Emily pressed her hand against her stomach which appeared to be turning somersaults. "We can be there in half an hour."

THE CAR HAD BEEN PARKED outside for ten minutes before Emily finally gathered up her courage and got out. Both Crystal and Gregory had been silent during her deliberation while Fred had stared at her with a full dose of petulance.

"Here goes nothing," she said, mostly for her own benefit, as she strode up to the front door. Net curtains were drawn over every window and she hoped somebody would be home, but it was impossible to see.

Three knocks and she stepped back, her calf muscles tensing as though to run. Fred stood beside her, an eager expression creeping across his face. Yearning.

"I don't think anybody—" she began, then cut off as footsteps sounded near the door. A lock clicked open, then another, then the handle turned. Everything moved into slow motion.

"Hey," a middle-aged woman said, leaning out with a half-smile.

Emily's voice disappeared for a second. She opened her mouth, but nothing came out.

"Are you selling something? Only, we're just in the middle of tea—"

"Is Wolfgang here?"

The woman's face had been edging into a frown, but it now cleared, and she stepped back. "Sure is. Just a sec. Wolfie," she yelled as she walked out through a doorway. In a more muffled tone. "There's a lady at the door for you."

Emily bit her lip at that. A lady. She thought the woman who'd answered must be her same age. Wolfgang would be too.

If he was the right man.

As soon as he appeared in the corridor, Emily knew she'd found the right target. On the online photos, there'd been a slight resemblance but in person, the similarities were striking.

Her eyes filled with tears of relief as she stood in the doorway, staring gormlessly at him and smiling.

"Can I help you?"

"You're Wolfgang? Your birth mother was Astrid Wall or Wallheimer?"

The man jerked his head around to check nobody was standing behind him, then pulled the door mostly closed, him on the outside with Emily. "Are you from the adoption agency? Do you have some news?"

Emily tried to think of a way to say what she had to without sounding like a madwoman. As she paused, Fred stepped forward, his hands reaching out towards the man standing there.

In a voice rusty with disuse, he said, "My son."

CHAPTER TWENTY-THREE

Wolfgang stepped out of the car and stared at the Stoneybrook Acres entrance. "It doesn't look evil."

"It's not." Emily came around to stand beside him. "I'm not even sure the people running it—now and in the past—could be classed that way. What's that book?" She snapped her fingers. "A series of unfortunate events. If you want to call it anything, unlucky would be a better title."

"It was certainly unlucky for my father."

"And by proxy, for you." Emily took his arm and steered him towards the oak tree rather than inside. The lawn was patchy, the lumps and chunks of broken concrete still piled near the wall. Where the police tape had been a week ago, now there was a temporary fence to protect the grass seed while it sprouted.

"I keep thinking if I'd just pushed the agency harder, I could've connected with my dad before he was gone."

Emily flicked her eyes towards where Fred stood, his eyes fixed in adoration on his son. "What would you have told him?"

"I don't know. Probably nothing." Wolfgang laughed and shook his head. "My wife accuses me of being monosyllabic at the best of times."

Under the tree, Emily stared at the wounded trunk with fresh eyes. The scars hadn't healed all the way—neither the ones sunk in the wood or the ones buried in the ground.

"The headmaster left all his money into a trust to be paid out to the children who survived Oakhaven School. It's not enough to make up for what he did, or how he covered it up, but I guess it shows, in the end, he felt guilt."

"Not much use for the ones who'd moved on to other cities."

Emily tapped on his arm. "Your father moved down here to take advantage of the offer. I don't know how or when the pupils were informed, but it brought him back here."

"To be killed."

"Yeah." Emily shifted her weight to her left side as her right hip raised a protest. The muscle at the back of her knee gave a twinge, and she clenched her teeth, ready for a cramp. After a second, they loosened again, offering a reprieve.

"I think he came to the house, once."

The admission took her so much by surprise that Emily gasped. "Really?"

Wolfgang nodded, looking bereft. "I think so. It was about two years ago. I was in the front room on the computer when he walked past and up to the door. I expected him to knock and my wife was closer, so I just kept on with what I was doing. About five minutes later, he walked past again. He never knocked or rang the bell."

The ghost reached out for his son, a hand passing

through his shoulder. Wolfgang shivered while Mr Wilmott trembled, tears streaming down his face.

"If only I'd gone to answer the door that day, so many things might've been different."

Emily stared at the ghost, biting her lip as she tried to find the words to heal the breach between them. "I think, if he was standing here now, he'd be proud to know you as his son."

Fred nodded. "When my friends died, I didn't just lose them, I lost any chance to get to Astrid and prove to her I could be a father. That was the plan. Get a job and support her and the baby. By the time Mr Leuf was finished with me and I got to the hospital, I was so traumatised I couldn't speak and the staff there couldn't work out what I wanted. They put me in an asylum for a while after that. Long enough so when I was discharged, I could barely remember anything that had happened."

"A string of bad luck might have kept the two of you apart," Emily said, stroking the tree trunk where the scars were deepest. "But I think if you talk now, he'd listen. No matter how far away he might go, I believe he'll hear you and be waiting."

They turned back toward the retirement complex but as they drew nearer, Wolfgang pulled away. "I don't want to go inside if that's all right. Maybe another day, now that I know it's here. Just not today."

Emily headed towards the car, but again the man shook his head. "There's a bus that goes by in less than ten minutes that'll have me home in an hour. I'm grateful for you showing me around, but I think I'd rather travel back on my own."

She waved to him as he walked down the winding driveway. Fred came and stood beside her, his posture an exact mimicry of his son.

"Why didn't I have the courage to knock that day? All those years, I held onto him as the one good thing that came out of my life. Just the knowledge that I had a son somewhere, made it easier to keep going."

Emily shrugged. "Sometimes we dream so hard, it's hard to believe the reality will come close. I don't even know if it's fear. It feels more like love."

"Freddie! You're it!"

The two of them turned to see the filled in burial plots bathed in radiant light. Three boys stood inside the brightness, gesturing to Frederick to join them.

"I want to stay." The ghost turned, his eyes searching the path his son had just walked. "What happens if I go? Will I ever see him again?"

"Cynthia doesn't have any problem coming back." Emily realised her hands were clenching as she said that and forced them to relax with a small laugh. "Peanut went and came back, too."

"Fred?"

This time, when they turned around, Astrid was standing there, waiting. She extended her hand and Frederick ran towards her, pulling her into his arms and twirling her around.

"Did you see him?" Fred asked, his voice thick with emotion. "Wolfgang?"

"I saw him. He turned out okay, considering his parents were *nothing but trouble*." Astrid spoke the last words in a plummy accent, perhaps imitating someone they both knew because Frederick burst into laughter.

"Will you come with me and be my love again?"

Mr Wilmott nodded, cupping her face in his hands as

the teenage boys bounced around them, catcalling. With a burst of energy, the light absorbed them.

"KNOCK, KNOCK," Emily said at Agnes's door, seeing it slightly ajar.

"Who's there?" a voice called out, female but not Agnes.

"Come in. Just watch you don't let the dogs out."

"*Who let the dogs out?*" a voice sang off-key, and Emily pushed inside, shutting the door behind her, to find Suzanne Wilberforce and Conker in the room.

"Am I interrupting something?" Emily asked.

"Yes," Agnes said from the head of the bed. "An argument about the relative merits of paint by numbers as opposed to needlework."

Maude trotted over to sniff at Emily's ankles, seemingly disappointed to discover there were no dog treats secreted in her socks.

"Poor lady," Suzanne said, snapping her fingers to call Maude over. "Some big meanie put her on a diet and now all the fun's gone from her life."

Agnes snorted. "She'll get over it. I was on a diet from the age of sixteen through sixty." She patted her ample hips. "For all the good it did me."

"To old age putting an end to fad diets," Suzanne said, raising a glass of what looked suspiciously like sherry, in a toast.

"Hear, hear." Agnes produced a glass she'd been concealing behind her back and took a large swig. "But Maude is just a spring chicken, aren't you darling? Only eight so in dog's years that's..."

"Just a bit older than me," Emily finished for her. "And I can tell you right now if you wanted to put *me* on a diet, you'd be out of luck."

Suzanne doubled over with laughter. To Emily, it looked like the glass wasn't the first of the day.

"Michael!" Agnes squealed with delight and shoved up the window. The painted wood caught at an angle and gave a matching shriek back.

"Hello stranger," Michael said to Emily, poking his head into the room. "I didn't expect to see you around here again."

"It's her favourite place because we're here," Suzanne announced, grabbing hold of Emily's hand. "She loves us and loves our dogs, so how could she stay away?"

"True enough," Michael said with a wink at Emily. "How could she resist such gorgeous ladies? Especially when they've spent the morning getting soused."

Agnes leaned out, placing a hand on his arm. "We're having an early tipple because the new owners are coming tomorrow, so we'll have to be on our best behaviour from now on."

"Ah. Better drink it all up today, then." He tapped a finger against his nose. "Good call."

"Speaking of people we didn't expect to see back here..." Emily stepped closer to the window.

"Oh." Michael clutched at his chest. "That's the worst segue I've heard in quite some time."

"Have you moved back in or are you just hanging around outside the windows, flirting?"

He waggled his eyebrows and mimed a cigar. "Can't it be both?" After a short pause with no response, he sighed. "Talk about a hard audience. I've moved back into my room, citing a mix-up with paperwork through no fault of my own.

Unfortunately, getting that changed into my real name means I don't qualify for the Samuel Leuf grant any longer. Luckily, I heard on the grapevine this place needed a new gardener."

Emily's face must have shown her shock in detail, because Michael laughed again, shaking his head.

"No, I can tell what you're thinking. I'm not too old and if there's anything I can't handle, I'll arrange for some work experience on the cheap." He wrinkled his nose. "I can work a system as well as the next man, and unlike the last employee, I'm not about to take an axe to the residents."

"Well, I still don't know why that horrid man hurt Freddie like that," Suzanne said with a sniff. "We didn't interact much, all I remember about him was that he wouldn't say boo to a ghost. Still, not being noisy doesn't seem a great reason to murder someone."

"Frederick attacked the gardener when Eli tried to chop down the oak tree." Emily moved back from the window, taking a seat on the bed next to Agnes. "It was an accident, but he panicked, from all accounts. Once he'd shoved the body into the shed, he spread a rumour that poor Mr Wilmott had wandered off into the rear field. Nobody had any reason to doubt him. He'd already dug out the ground for the patio so disposing of him was a quick fix."

"You get that from your police friend?" Agnes asked, her eyes suddenly on full alert.

"I got that from the sergeant, yes. I wouldn't—"

"Ooh!" Suzanne interrupted in a falsetto. "I wouldn't call him a friend. More of an acquaintance or a colleague. We're definitely not making eyes at each other over crime scenes. No, not at all."

Emily's mouth dropped open in horror. "But... I..."

"I wouldn't worry, love," Michael called from the

window. "You think the gossip in a small town is bad, you don't want to see what they get up to in here." He rolled his eyes. "The rumours I've heard!"

Thinking there was no time like the present, Emily escaped the room, Maude's sad and hungry eyes following her. She walked through the centre of the retirement complex and past the nurse's station where two women she'd never seen before were on duty.

Gladys stood by the window and gestured for Emily to come and join her. When she gazed out through the glass, the lingering mist of light from Mr Wilmott's exit was still floating near the side of the building.

"I always said he'd meet up with her again, one day," she said to Emily, taking her hand and squeezing it between both of hers. "He always shook his head, thinking he'd lost his chance, but I knew I was right."

"You were." Emily stared across the grounds towards the oak tree. "I wonder if they'll take that thing down, now."

"I dare say it's already had its full of schoolboys," Gladys said in a voice losing its tenuous hold on the present. "Grab the axe and chop it down. The headmaster should've kept going when he had the chance."

"If you're a visitor, I hope you've signed in at reception," a stern voice said from behind them.

Emily jumped and turned, a thousand excuses ready on her lips. Then she saw who it was and relaxed. "Rebecca. I didn't think I'd see you in here again."

"I'm not here in my official capacity," the woman said, pulling up her trouser leg to reveal a monitoring bracelet with a steady red light. "But my community service overseer was kind enough to let this be one of the places I serve out my sentence."

Emily was taken aback. "I didn't realise you'd already gone through the court system."

Rebecca laughed at her surprise. "Everything's quicker when you plead guilty and agree to give evidence against those who don't have the good sense to. I was held inside for a couple of nights, then fitted with this wee fella"—she flashed her ankle again—"and given a list of places I could serve my time."

"What good luck." Emily shifted her weight from one foot to the other. "For you and for the residents here."

"It's nice to be back here," she agreed. "Except I keep getting asked for medication."

"I've got something for the people on this ward," Emily said, opening up her bulging handbag and pulling out a stack of games. "These belonged to my parents and they just about played them ragged when I was younger. I hoped the residents here might find some use for them."

Rebecca took the boxes, sorting through the different titles with an occasional nostalgic sigh. "I'm sure they'll love them. I'll set a few of them up in the common room and see who takes a fancy."

Gladys followed Rebecca through into the room, clapping her hands in time to her steps. As Emily wound her way back through the corridors, she felt more confident about the thought of coming here in the future.

Stoneybrook Acres would do her well enough.

As she walked out through reception, Emily nodded goodbye to the young woman on duty, who looked flustered enough for it to be her first day.

Halfway to the car, Michael caught up with her. "I didn't want you to go without properly thanking you," he said, rubbing a hand up the back of his neck. "That day up the tree, I was half-crazy. If you hadn't talked me down…"

"I hope you would've seen sense either way." Emily folded her arms across her chest, feeling as though she was made of elbows and knees. "There's a lot of people around here would've missed you."

"Yeah, I guess." He paused for a second, then beamed his usual broad smile. "I'm glad to be sorted, with everyone calling me by my proper name. Another few months of that, and I swear I'd have forgotten who I was for real."

"I'm glad they're not pressing charges."

"Oh, they still might." Michael scrunched up his nose and scratched behind his ear. "I'm not sure what, exactly, but Sergeant Winchester warned me not to leave town."

"You mean, my boyfriend?"

He burst into laughter and gave her a slap on the back. "Well, I hope not. Either way, come back soon, yeah? There're not many folks in here who can keep up with me if you know what I mean."

Emily didn't, but she was also too shy to ask. As she waved goodbye, her gaze travelled over the rough patches on the lawn, small green shoots beginning to sprout up already.

Life kept trucking on, no matter what got thrown at it.

"Get a move on," she warned herself, turning the key and putting the car in reverse. "You'll be here for good soon enough. Time to get out and live it up while you can."

Blueberries and Bereavement (Sweet Baked Mystery)

Strawberries and Suffering (Sweet Baked Mystery)

Cupcakes and Conspiracies (Sweet Baked Mystery)

Food Bowl Mysteries Books 1-3

You're Kitten Me (Food Bowl Mystery)

Cat Red-Handed (Food Bowl Mystery)

An Impawsible Situation (Food Bowl Mystery)

The Only Secret Left to Keep (Detective Ngaire Blakes)

The Second Stage of Grief (Detective Ngaire Blakes)

The Three Deaths of Magdalene Lynton (Detective Ngaire Blakes)

Christchurch Crime Thriller Boxset

Breathe and Release (A Christchurch Crime Thriller)

Skeletal (A Christchurch Crime Thriller)

Found, Near Water (A Christchurch Crime Thriller)

Katherine Hayton is a middle-aged woman who works in insurance, doesn't have children or pets, can't drive, has lived in Christchurch her entire life, and currently resides a two-minute walk from where she was born.

For some reason, she's developed a rich fantasy life.

www.katherinehayton.com

9 780995 100749